KT-483-519

Truly Scary Stories for Fearless Kids

Truly Scary Stories for Fearless Kids

KEY PORTER BOOKS

CLD 21688. This edition published in 2001 for Colour Library Direct Ltd,
New Mill, New Mill Lane, Witney, Oxon, 0X8 5TF

Canadian Cataloguing in Publication Data
Main entry under title:
Truly scary stories for fearless kids
Includes bibliographical references.
ISBN 1-55013-994-0
1. Children's stories. I. Slavin, Bill. II. Weissmann, Joe, 1947- .
PZ5.T784 1998 j808.83'1 C98-930879-0

The publisher gratefully acknowledges the support of the Canada Council for the Arts and the Ontario Arts Council for its publishing program.

Key Porter Books Limited
70 The Esplanade
Toronto, Ontario
Canada M5E 1R2

Illustrations on pages 3, 10, 13, 18, 22, 40, 43, 44, 47, 54, 57, 59, 60, 66, 69, 71, 88, 102, 105, 107, 126, 130, 135, 137, 140, 165, 182, 187, 195, 217, 218, 222, 226, 238, 241, 246, 252, are by Joe Weissmann; those on pages 24, 27, 30, 34, 38, 39, 50, 53, 65, 74, 81, 84, 86, 89, 90, 93, 94, 99, 109, 110, 113, 115, 120, 123, 142, 146, 154, 157, 158, 160, 162, 166, 168, 175, 176, 179, 197, 198, 203, 210, 214, 228, 230, 235, 256, 258, 263, 267, are by Bill Slavin.

Electronic Formatting: Heidi Palfrey

Printed and bound in Spain

01 6 5 4 3 2 1

Contents

Jimmy Takes Vanishing Lessons

WALTER R. BROOKS

The school bus picked up Jimmy Crandall every morning at the side road that led up to his aunt's house, and every afternoon it dropped him there again. And so twice a day, on the bus, he passed the entrance to the mysterious road.

It wasn't much of a road any more. It was choked with weeds and blackberry bushes, and the woods on both sides pressed in so closely that the branches met overhead, and it was dark and gloomy even on bright days. The bus driver once pointed it out.

"Folks that go in there after dark," he said, "well, they usually don't ever come out again. There's a haunted house about a quarter of a mile down the road." He paused. "But you ought to know about that, Jimmy. It was your grandfather's house."

Jimmy knew about it, and he knew that it now belonged to his Aunt Mary. But Jimmy's aunt would never talk to him about the house. She said the stories about it were silly nonsense and there were no such things as ghosts. If all the villagers weren't a lot of superstitious idiots, she would be able to rent the house, and

then she would have enough money to buy Jimmy some decent clothes and take him to the movies.

Jimmy thought it was all very well to say that there were no such things as ghosts, but how about the people who had tried to live there? Aunt Mary had rented the house three times, but every family had moved out within a week. They said the things that went on there were just too queer. So nobody would live in it any more.

Jimmy thought about the house a lot. If he could only prove that there wasn't a ghost.... And one Saturday when his aunt was in the village, Jimmy took the key to the haunted house from its hook on the kitchen door and started out.

It had seemed like a fine idea when he had first thought of it—to find out for himself. Even in the silence and damp gloom of the old road it still seemed pretty good. Nothing to be scared of, he told himself. Ghosts aren't around in the daytime. But when he came out in the clearing and looked at those blank, dusty windows, he wasn't so sure.

"Oh, come on!" he told himself. And he squared his shoulders and waded through the long grass to the porch.

Then he stopped again. His feet did not seem to want to go up the steps. It took him nearly five minutes to persuade them to move. But when at last they did, they marched right up and across the porch to the front door, and Jimmy set his teeth hard and put the key in the keyhole. It turned with a squeak. He pushed the door open and went in.

That was probably the bravest thing that Jimmy had ever done. He was in a long dark hall with closed doors on both sides, and on the right the stairs went up. He had left the door open behind him, and the light from it showed him that, except for the hatrack and table and chairs, the hall was empty. And then as he stood there, listening to the bumping of his heart, gradually the light faded, the hall grew darker and darker—as if something huge had come up

on the porch behind him and stood there, blocking the doorway. He swung round quickly, but there was nothing there.

He drew a deep breath. It must have been just a cloud passing across the sun. But then the door, all of itself, began to swing shut. And before he could stop it, it closed with a bang. And it was then, as he was pulling frantically at the handle to get out, that Jimmy saw the ghost.

It behaved just as you would expect a ghost to behave. It was a tall, dim, white figure, and it came gliding slowly down the stairs towards him. Jimmy gave a yell, yanked the door open, and tore down the steps.

He didn't stop until he was well down the road. Then he had

to get his breath. He sat down on a log. "Boy!" he said. "I've seen a ghost! Golly, was that awful!" Then after a minute, he thought, "What was so awful about it? He was trying to scare me, like that smart Alec who was always jumping out from behind things. Pretty silly business for a grown-up ghost to be doing."

It always makes you mad when someone deliberately tries to scare you. And as Jimmy got over his fright, he began to get angry. And pretty soon he got up and started back. "I must get that key, anyway," he thought, for he had left it in the door.

This time he approached very quietly. He thought he'd just lock the door and go home. But as he tiptoed up the steps he saw it was still open; and as he reached out cautiously for the key, he heard a faint sound. He drew back and peeked around the doorjamb, and there was the ghost.

The ghost was going back upstairs, but he wasn't gliding now, he was doing a sort of dance, and every other step he would bend double and shake with laughter. His thin cackle was the sound Jimmy had heard. Evidently he was enjoying the joke he had played. That made Jimmy madder than ever. He stuck his head farther around the doorjamb and yelled "Boo!" at the top of his lungs. The ghost gave a thin shriek and leaped two feet in the air, then collapsed on the stairs.

As soon as Jimmy saw he could scare the ghost even worse than the ghost could scare him, he wasn't afraid any more, and he came right into the hall. The ghost was hanging on to the banisters and panting. "Oh, my goodness!" he gasped. "Oh, my gracious! Boy, you can't *do* that to me!"

"I did it, didn't I?" said Jimmy. "Now we're even."

"Nothing of the kind," said the ghost crossly. "You seem pretty stupid, even for a boy. Ghosts are supposed to scare people. People aren't supposed to scare ghosts." He got up slowly and glided down and sat on the bottom step. "But look here, boy; this could be pretty serious for me if people got to know about it."

"You mean you don't want me to tell anybody about it?" Jimmy asked.

"Suppose we make a deal," the ghost said. "You keep still about this, and in return I'll—well, let's see; how would you like to know how to vanish?"

"Oh, that would be swell!" Jimmy exclaimed. "But—can you vanish?"

"Sure," said the ghost, and he did. All at once he just wasn't there. Jimmy was alone in the hall.

But his voice went right on. "It would be pretty handy, wouldn't it?" he said persuasively. "You could get into the movies free whenever you wanted to, and if your aunt called you to do something—when you were in the yard, say—well, she wouldn't be able to find you."

"I don't mind helping Aunt Mary," Jimmy said.

"H'm. High-minded, eh?" said the ghost. "Well, then—"

"I wish you'd please reappear," Jimmy interrupted. "It makes me feel funny to talk to somebody who isn't there."

"Sorry, I forgot," said the ghost, and there he was again, sitting on the bottom step. Jimmy could see the step, dimly, right through him. "Good trick, eh? Well, if you don't like vanishing, maybe I could teach you to seep through keyholes. Like this." He floated over to the door and went right through the keyhole, the way water goes down the drain. Then he came back the same way.

"That's useful, too," he said. "Getting into locked rooms and so on. You can go anywhere the wind can."

"No," said Jimmy. "There's only one thing you can do to get me to promise not to tell about scaring you. Go live somewhere else. There's Miller's, up the road. Nobody lives there any more."

"That old shack!" said the ghost, with a nasty laugh. "Doors and windows half off, roof leaky—no thanks! What do you think it's like in a storm, windows banging, rain dripping on you—I guess not! Peace and quiet, that's really what a ghost wants out of life."

"Well, I don't think it's very fair," Jimmy said, "for you to live in a house that doesn't belong to you and keep my aunt from renting it."

"Pooh!" said the ghost. "I'm not stopping her from renting it. I don't take up any room, and it's not my fault if people get scared and leave."

"It certainly is!" Jimmy said angrily. "You don't play fair and I'm not going to make any bargain with you. I'm going to tell everybody how I scared you."

"Oh, you mustn't do that!" The ghost seemed quite disturbed and he vanished and reappeared rapidly several times. "If that got out, every ghost in the country would be in terrible trouble."

So they argued about it. The ghost said if Jimmy wanted money he could learn to vanish; then he could join a circus and get a big salary. Jimmy said he didn't want to be in a circus; he wanted to go to college and learn to be a doctor. He was very firm. And the ghost began to cry. "But this is my *home,* boy," he said. "Thirty years I've lived here and no trouble to anybody, and now you want to throw me out into the cold world! And for what? A little money! That's pretty heartless." And he sobbed, trying to make Jimmy feel cruel.

Jimmy didn't feel cruel at all, for the ghost had certainly driven plenty of other people out into the cold world. But he didn't really think it would do much good for him to tell anybody that he had scared the ghost. Nobody would believe him, and how could he prove it? So after a minute he said, "Well, all right. You teach me to vanish and I won't tell." They settled it that way.

Jimmy didn't say anything to his aunt about what he'd done. But every Saturday he went to the haunted house for his vanishing lesson. It is really quite easy when you know how, and in a couple of weeks he could flicker, and in six weeks the ghost gave him an examination and he got a B plus, which is very good for a human. So he thanked the ghost and shook hands with him and said, "Well, good-bye now. You'll hear from me."

"What do you mean by that?" said the ghost suspiciously. But Jimmy just laughed and ran off home.

That night at supper Jimmy's aunt said, "Well, what have you been doing today?"

"I've been learning to vanish."

His aunt smiled and said, "That must be fun."

"Honestly," said Jimmy. "The ghost up at grandfather's taught me."

"I don't think that's very funny," said his aunt. "And will you please not—why, where are you?" she demanded, for he had vanished.

"Here, Aunt Mary," he said, as he reappeared.

"Merciful heavens!" she exclaimed, and she pushed back her chair and rubbed her eyes hard. Then she looked at him again.

Well it took a lot of explaining and he had to do it twice more before he could persuade her that he really could vanish. She was pretty upset. But at last she calmed down and they had a long talk. Jimmy kept his word and didn't tell her that he had scared the ghost, but he said he had a plan, and at last, though very reluctantly, she agreed to help him.

So the next day she went up to the old house and started to work. She opened the windows and swept and dusted and aired the bedding, and made as much noise as possible. This disturbed the ghost, and pretty soon he came floating into the room where

she was sweeping. She was scared all right. She gave a yell and threw the broom at him. As the broom went right through him and he came nearer, waving his arms and groaning, she shrank back.

And Jimmy, who had been standing there invisible all the time, suddenly appeared and jumped at the ghost with a "Boo!" And the ghost fell over in a dead faint.

As soon as Jimmy's aunt saw that, she wasn't frightened any more. She found some smelling salts and held them under the ghost's nose, and when he came to she tried to help him into a chair. Of course she couldn't help him much because her hands went right through him. But at last he sat up and said reproachfully to Jimmy, "You broke your word!"

"I promised not to tell about scaring you," said the boy, "but I didn't promise not to scare you again."

And his aunt said, "You really are a ghost, aren't you? I thought you were just stories people made up. Well, excuse me, but I must get on with my work." And she began sweeping and banging around with her broom harder than ever.

The ghost put his hands to his head. "All this noise," he said. "Couldn't you work more quietly, ma'am?"

"Whose house is this, anyway?" she demanded. "If you don't like it, why don't you move out?"

The ghost sneezed violently several times. "Excuse me," he said. "You're raising so much dust. Where's that boy?" he asked suddenly. For Jimmy had vanished again.

"I'm sure I don't know," she replied. "Probably getting ready to scare you again."

"You ought to have better control of him," said the ghost severely. "If he was my boy, I'd take a hairbrush to him."

"You have my permission," she said, and she reached right through the ghost and pulled the chair cushion out from under him and began banging the dust out of it. "What's more," she went on, as he got up and glided wearily to another chair, "Jimmy and I are going to sleep here nights from now on, and I don't think it would be very smart of you to try any tricks."

"Ha, ha," said the ghost nastily. "He who laughs last—"

"Ha, ha, yourself," said Jimmy's voice from close behind him. "And that's me, laughing last."

The ghost muttered and vanished.

Jimmy's aunt put cotton in her ears and slept that night in the best bedroom with the light lit. The ghost screamed for a while down in the cellar, but nothing happened, so he came upstairs. He thought he would appear to her as two glaring, fiery eyes, which was one of his best tricks, but first he wanted to be sure where Jimmy was. But he couldn't find him. He hunted all over the house, and though he was invisible himself, he got more and more nervous. He kept imagining that at any moment Jimmy might jump out at him from some dark corner and scare him into fits. Finally he got so jittery that he went back to the cellar and hid in the coal bin all night.

The following days were just as bad for the ghost. Several times he tried to scare Jimmy's aunt while she was working, but she didn't scare worth a cent, and twice Jimmy managed to sneak up on him and appear suddenly with a loud yell, frightening him dreadfully. He was, I suppose, rather timid even for a ghost. He began to look quite haggard. He had several long arguments with Jimmy's aunt, in which he wept and appealed to her sympathy, but she was firm. If he wanted to live there he would have to pay rent, just like anybody else. There was the abandoned Miller farm two miles up the road. Why didn't he move there?

When the house was all in apple-pie order, Jimmy's aunt went down to the village to see a Mr. and Mrs. Whistler, who were living at the hotel because they couldn't find a house to move into. She told them about the old house, but they said "No, thank you. We've heard about that house. It's haunted. I'll bet," they said, "*you* wouldn't dare spend a night there."

She told them that she had spent the last week there, but they evidently didn't believe her. So she said, "You know my nephew, Jimmy. He's twelve years old. I am so sure that the house is not haunted that, if you want to rent it, I will let Jimmy stay there with you every night until you are sure everything is all right."

"Ha!" said Mr. Whistler. "The boy won't do it. He's got more sense."

So they sent for Jimmy. "Why, I've spent the last week there," he said. "Sure. I'd just as soon."

But the Whistlers still refused.

So Jimmy's aunt went around and told a lot of the village people about their talk, and everybody made so much fun of the Whistlers for being afraid, when a twelve-year-old boy wasn't, that they were ashamed, and said they would rent it. So they moved in. Jimmy stayed there for a week, but he saw nothing of the ghost. And then one day one of the boys in his grade told him that somebody had seen a ghost up at the Miller farm. So Jimmy knew the ghost had taken his aunt's advice.

A day or two later he walked up to the Miller farm. There was no front door and he walked right in. There was some groaning and thumping upstairs, and then after a minute the ghost came floating down.

"Oh, it's you!" he said. "Goodness sakes, boy, can't you leave me in peace?"

Jimmy said he'd just come up to see how he was getting along.

"Getting along fine," said the ghost. "From my point of view it's a very desirable property. Peaceful. Quiet. Nobody playing silly tricks."

"Well," said Jimmy, "I won't bother you if you don't bother the Whistlers. But if you come back there—"

"Don't worry," said the ghost.

So with the rent money, Jimmy and his aunt had a much easier life. They went to the movies sometimes twice a week, and Jimmy had all new clothes, and on Thanksgiving, for the first time in his life, Jimmy had a turkey. Once a week he would go up to the Miller farm to see the ghost and they got to be very good friends. The ghost even came down to the Thanksgiving dinner, though of course he couldn't eat much. He seemed to enjoy the warmth of the house and he was in very good humor. He taught Jimmy several more tricks. The best one was how to glare with fiery eyes, which was useful later on when Jimmy became a doctor and had

to look down people's throats to see if their tonsils ought to come out. He was really a pretty good fellow as ghosts go, and Jimmy's aunt got quite fond of him herself. When the real winter weather began, she even used to worry about him a lot, because of course there was no heat in the Miller place and the doors and windows didn't amount to much and there was hardly any roof. The ghost tried to explain to her that heat and cold didn't bother ghosts at all.

"Maybe not," she said, "but just the same, it can't be very pleasant." And when he accepted their invitation for Christmas dinner she knitted some red woollen slippers, and he was so

pleased that he broke down and cried. And that made Jimmy's aunt so happy, *she* broke down and cried.

Jimmy didn't cry, but he said, "Aunt Mary, don't you think it would be nice if the ghost came down and lived with us this winter?"

"I would feel very much better about him if he did," she said.

So he stayed with them that winter, and then he just stayed on, and it must have been a peaceful place for the last I heard he was still there.

Of a Promise Kept

LAFCADIO HEARN

"I shall return in the early autumn," said Akana Soyëmon several hundred years ago when bidding goodbye to his brother by adoption, young Hasébé Samon. The time was spring, and the place was the village of Kato in the province of Harima. Akana was an Izumo samurai, and he wanted to visit his birthplace.

Hasébé said, "Your Izumo, the Country of the Eight-Cloud Rising, is very distant. Perhaps it will therefore be difficult for you to promise to return here upon any particular day. But if we were to know the exact day, we should feel happier. We could then prepare a feast of welcome and we could watch at the gateway for your coming."

"Why, as for that," responded Akana, "I have been so much accustomed to travel that I can usually tell beforehand how long it will take me to reach a place, and I can safely promise you to be here upon a particular day. Suppose we say the day of the festival Choyo?"

"That is the ninth day of the ninth month," said Hasébé. "Then the chrysanthemums will be in bloom, and we can go together to look at them. How pleasant! ... So you promise to come back on the ninth day of the ninth month?"

"On the ninth day of the ninth month," repeated Akana, smiling farewell. Then he strode away from the village of Kato in the province of Harima—and Hasébé Samon and the mother of Hasébé looked after him with tears in their eyes.

"Neither the Sun nor the Moon," says an old Japanese proverb, "ever halt upon their journey." Swiftly the months went by, and the autumn came—the season of chrysanthemums. And early upon the morning of the ninth day of the ninth month Hasébé prepared to welcome his adopted brother. He made ready a feast of good things, bought wine, decorated the guestroom, and filled the vases of the alcove with chrysanthemums of two colors. Then his mother, watching him, said, "The province of Izumo, my son, is more than one hundred ri from this place, and the journey thence over the mountains is difficult and weary, and you cannot be sure that Akana will be able to come today. Would it not be better, before you take all this trouble, to wait for his coming?"

"Nay, mother!" Hasébé made answer, "Akana promised to be here today: he could not break a promise! And if he were to see us beginning to make preparation after his arrival, he would know that we had doubted his word, and we should be put to shame."

The day was beautiful, the sky without a cloud, and the air so pure that the world seemed to be a thousand miles wider than usual. In the morning many travelers passed through the village—some of them samurai. Hasébé, watching each as he came, more than once imagined that he saw Akana approaching. But the temple bells sounded the hour of midday, and Akana did not appear. Through the afternoon also Hasébé watched and waited in vain. The sun set, and still there was no sign of Akana. Nevertheless Hasébé remained at the gate, gazing down the road. Later his mother went to him and said, "The mind of a man, my son—as our proverb declares—may change as quickly as the sky of autumn. But your chrysanthemum flowers will still be fresh tomorrow.

Better now to sleep, and in the morning you can watch again for Akana, if you wish."

"Rest well, mother," returned Hasébé, "but I still believe that he will come." Then the mother went to her own room, and Hasébé lingered at the gate.

The night was pure as the day had been: all the sky throbbed with stars, and the white River of Heaven shimmered with unusual splendor. The village slept; the silence was broken only by the noise of a little brook and by the faraway barking of peasants' dogs. Hasébé still waited—waited until he saw the thin moon sink behind the neighboring hills. Then at last he began to doubt and to fear. Just as he was about to reenter the house, he perceived in the distance a tall man approaching—very lightly and quickly; and in the next moment he recognized Akana.

"Oh!" cried Hasébé, springing to meet him—"I have been waiting for you from the morning until now! . . . So you really did keep your promise after all. . . . But you must be tired, poor brother! Come in—everything is ready for you." He guided Akana to the place of honor in the guestroom, and hastened to trim the lights, which were burning low. "Mother," continued Hasébé, "felt a little tired this evening, and she has already gone to bed; but I shall awaken her presently." Akana shook his head and made a little gesture of disapproval. "As you will, brother," said Hasébé; and he set warm food and wine before the traveler. Akana did not touch the food or the wine, but remained motionless and silent for a short time. Then, speaking in a whisper—as if fearful of awakening the mother, he said:

"Now I must tell you how it happened that I came thus late. When I returned to Izumo I found that the people had almost forgotten the kindness of our former ruler, the good Lord Enya, and were seeking the favor of the usurper Tsunéhisa, who had possessed himself of the Tonda Castle. But I had to visit my cousin, Akana Tanji, though he had accepted service under Tsunéhisa, and was living, as a retainer, within the castle grounds. He persuaded me to present myself before Tsunéhisa: I yielded chiefly in order to observe the character of the new ruler, whose face I had never seen. He is a skilled soldier, and of great courage, but he is cunning and cruel. I found it necessary to let him know that I could never enter into his service. After I left his presence he ordered my cousin to detain me—to keep me confined within the house. I protested that I had promised to return to Harima upon the ninth day of the ninth month, but I was refused permission to go. I then hoped to escape from the castle at night, but I was constantly watched, and until today I could find no way to fulfill my promise."

"Until today!" exclaimed Hasébé in bewilderment. "The castle is more than a hundred ri from here!"

"Yes," returned Akana, "And no living man can travel on foot a hundred ri in one day. But I felt that if I did not keep my promise, you could not think well of me. And I remembered the ancient proverb. "*Tama yoku ichi nichi ni sen ri wo yuku.*" (The soul of a man can journey a thousand ri in a day.) Fortunately I had been allowed to keep my sword—thus only was I able to come to you.... Be good to our mother."

With these words he stood up, and in the same instant disappeared.

Then Hasébé knew that Akana had killed himself in order to fulfill the promise.

At earliest dawn Hasébé Samon set out for the Castle Tonda, in the province of Izumo. Reaching Matsué, he there learned that, on the night of the ninth day of the ninth month, Akana Soyëmon had performed harakiri in the house of Akana Tanji, in the grounds of the castle. Then Hasébé went to the house of Akana Tanji and reproached Akana Tanji for the treachery done, and slew him in the midst of his family, and escaped without hurt. And when the Lord Tsunéhisa had heard the story, he gave commands that Hasébé should not be pursued. For, although an unscrupulous and cruel man himself, the Lord Tsunéhisa could respect the love of truth in others, and could admire the friendship and the courage of Hasébé Samon.

The Storm

JULES VERNE

In 1863 the thirty-five-year-old Jules Verne walked into the offices of publisher Pierre Hetzel and told him about his idea for his first book: Five Weeks in a Balloon. *Hetzel listened, first politely, then interested, finally spellbound. When Verne had finished, Hetzel asked him if he had any more ideas for these "scientific adventure stories," as Verne called them. Timidly, but with increasing confidence, Jules Verne told Hetzel of his imaginary travels. That afternoon Verne took Hetzel deep under the sea, away to the moon, into the heart of darkest India, down to the center of the Earth. The interview ended with a twenty-year contract for three books a year. Hetzel then decided to create a deluxe series on the strength of his faith in his unknown writer's imagination, and one of the world's best-beloved authors was launched on his career.*

"The Storm" is unlike anything else I have read by Jules Verne. Usually his novels and stories are straightforward tales of adventure in which a scientific explanation is given to a seemingly fantastic occurrence. In "The Storm" nothing is explained; the reader is left with a sense of vertigo not easily dispelled.

The wind is blowing. The rain is pouring down. The roaring storm bends the trees on the Volsinian shore and crashes against the flanks of the Crimma Mountains. On the coast, the high rocks are relentlessly gnawed away by the sharp teeth of the Megalocridian Sea.

Deep within the shelter of the bay lies the little village of Luktrop—barely a few hundred houses whose green belvederes try vainly to defend themselves from the ocean winds. Four or five narrow streets climb the mountainside, looking more like gullies than streets, paved with pebbles and choked with rubble spat from the eruptive cone that rises in the background. The Vanglor volcano is not far away. During the day the inner cauldron releases sulphur fumes. At night, at regular intervals, it spews forth long flames. Visible at a distance of a hundred and fifty *kertses*, like a lighthouse, the Vanglor pinpoints the port of Luktrop to coasting vessels, *felzane* ships, *verley* boats and even light *balanzes* whose bows cut through the icy Megalocridian waters.

At the far end of the village, next to a handful of Crimmerian ruins, are the Arab quarters: a casbah with whitewashed walls, round roofs and terraces gobbled up by the sun. The Casbah resembles a pile of stone cubes, of dice with the edges worn thin by time.

Among the notable buildings of Luktrop is the Six-Four, a bizarre construction with a square roof, six windows at the front and four at the back. A steeple dominates the village: the square tower of Saint Philifenus, whose bells are tolling in the storm. When this happens the villagers tremble with fear. "An evil omen!" they say.

This is Luktrop. Farther away—but not far—are a few miserable hovels scattered around the village in a landscape of bushes and ferns, somewhat like Britanny. But this is not Britanny.

Someone has knocked discreetly on the narrow door of Six-Four, at the left-hand corner of Messagliere Street. It is certainly one of the most comfortable houses in the village—if the word can be used when referring to Luktrop; one of the richest—if earning a few thousand *fretzers* can be considered a sign of wealth.

The knock has been answered by a savage snarl—something like the barking of a wolf. A window is raised above the Six-Four entrance.

"Go to hell, you nuisance, whoever you may be!" cries out an ill-humored voice.

A young girl, shivering under the rain, wrapped in a tattered shawl, asks whether Doctor Trifulgas is in.

"Maybe yes, maybe no; it all depends."

"It's about my father, he's dying!"

"Where is he dying?"

"Near Val Karniou, some four *kertses* from here."

"And his name?"

"Vort Kartif."

A hard man, this Doctor Trifulgas, not very compassionate. He only sees a patient after receiving payment in cash. Old Hurzof, the doctor's dog, half bulldog and half spaniel, has probably got a kinder heart. Six-Four only opens its doors to the rich. Every illness has a fixed price: one for curing typhoid fever, another for a cold, yet another for pericarditis or other such diseases which doctors invent by the dozen. Vort Kartif is a poor man, born of a poor family. Why should Doctor Trifulgas bother, especially on a night like this?

"Just getting me out of bed would have cost her ten *fretzers*!" he mutters, and lies down again.

Some twenty minutes later the iron knocker is heard once more. With a curse the doctor leaves his bed for the second time and leans out of the window.

"Who's there?" he cries.

"I'm Vort Kartif's wife."

"Vort Kartif of Val Karniou?"

"Yes, and if you refuse to come he'll die!"

"Fine, then you'll be a widow."

"Here are twenty *fretzers*—"

"Twenty *fretzers* to go all the way to Val Karniou, four *kertses* away?"

"For pity's sake!'

"Go to hell!"

And the window slams shut. Twenty *fretzers*! *What a fortune*! To risk catching a cold for twenty *fretzers*, especially when he is expected in Kiltreno tomorrow to look after rich Mr Edzingov's gout at fifty *fretzers* a visit!

With this happy thought, Doctor Trifulgas falls into a deeper sleep than before.

The beating of the storm is suddenly joined by three knocks on the door, this time from a firmer hand. The doctor is asleep. He wakes up, but in what a mood! Through the open window the storm enters like the blast of a machine gun.

"It's about Vort Kartif—"

"Not again!"

"I'm his mother!"

"May his mother, his wife and his daughter perish with him!"

"He's had a seizure!"

"So let him fight back!"

"We've been given some money on the house; we're selling it to Dontrup on Messagliere Street. But if you don't come now my grand-daughter won't have a father, my daughter-in-law won't have husband, and I won't have a son!"

It is pitiful and terrible to hear the old woman's voice, to imagine the wind freezing her blood and the rain soaking her thin flesh to the bones.

"A seizure is two hundred *fretzers*!" answers the heartless Trifulgas.

"We only have a hundred and twenty!"

"Good night!"

And the window closes once more.

However, after some careful thought, he concludes that a hundred and twenty *fretzers* for an hour and a half's walk, plus half an hour's visit, is about sixty *fretzers* an hour—a *fretzer* a minute. A small profit, yet not to be neglected.

Instead of going back to bed, the doctor puts on his outdoor clothes, his heavy marsh-boots, his fur cape, his woollen hood and his warm mittens. He leaves the lamp burning next to his *Codex* open at page 197. Then he pushes the door of Six-Four and steps outside.

The old woman is still there, leaning on her stick, wasted by her eighty years of misery.

"The hundred and twenty *fretzers*?"

"Here, here ... and may God make them a thousand in your pocket!"

"God! God's money! Has anyone ever seen God's money?"

The doctor whistles for Hurzof, hangs a small lamp from the brute's mouth, and takes the road towards the sea.

The old woman follows.

What weather, my God, what weather! The bells of Saint Philifenus are tolling in the wind: a bad sign. But Doctor Trifulgas is not superstitious. In fact he believes in nothing, not even in science—except in the profit it makes.

What weather! And what a road! Pebbles and rubble, rubble and pebbles. Pebbles slippery with seaweed, rubble that crackles like slag. No light except the one carried by Hurzof, dim and faltering. Sometimes they see Vanglor's leaping flames in which quaint figures seem to struggle.

The doctor and the old woman follow the pattern of small inlets that form the coast. The sea looks white, livid, mourning-white. It dazzles the eye as it shatters against the phosphorescent rim of the surf, spilling bucketfuls of glistening worms on to the strand.

Both figures continue to climb until the road turns between soft dunes where the broom and the reeds are thrown against each other by the wind with the click of bayonets. Here the old woman stops, and with a trembling finger points to a reddish light in the shadows. Vort Kartif's house.

"There?" asks the doctor.

"Yes," answers the woman.

The dog howls.

Suddenly the Vanglor shakes to its very roots. A sheaf of flames sprouts up into the sky, cleaving the clouds. Doctor Trifulgas falls backwards.

He swears like a damned soul. Then he scrambles to his feet and looks around him. The old woman is no longer there. Has she been swallowed by a gap in the ground or has she disappeared into the booming clouds? The dog is still there, sitting on its hind legs, the extinguished lamp still hanging from its mouth.

"Cowards," grumbles Doctor Trifulgas.

The honest man has received his hundred and twenty *fretzers*: now he feels he must earn them.

The small dot of light is about half a *kertse* away. The dying man's lamp ... the *dead* man's lamp, perhaps ... There is his house, as the old woman pointed out. There is no mistaking it.

Beneath the whistling wind, the beating rain, the rolling storm, Doctor Trifulgas marches on with hasty steps. As he advances, the house becomes clearer, standing alone in the middle of the heath. It looks a little like the doctor's house, Six-Four, in Luktrop. Same windows at the front, same narrow door ...

Doctor Trifulgas hurries on as fast as the wind will allow him. The door is ajar, he has only to push. He pushes, he steps inside, and the wind slams it shut behind his back.

Outside, Hurzof the dog starts to howl once again, pausing at regular intervals, like a cantor between the versicles of a psalm.

How very odd! It is almost as if Doctor Trifulgas had returned to his own house. However, he is certain he has not lost his way, he has not turned back. He is now in Val Karniou, not in Luktrop. And yet here is the same corridor, low and vaulted, the same wooden spiral staircase with its heavy handrail worn down by the palms of many hands ...

He climbs it. He arrives on the landing. A faint beam shines softly under the chamber door.

Is it his imagination? In the weak light he recognizes his own room, the yellow sofa to the right, the pearwood cupboard to the left, the steel-banded chest where he would have put his hundred and twenty *fretzers*. Here is his leather-patched armchair, here his bandy-legged table, and here, next to the dying lamp, his *Codex* open at page 197.

"What is happening to me?" he says in a low voice.

Doctor Trifulgas is afraid. His eyes shine wide open, his body seems contracted, diminished. A cold sweat runs down him. He is trembling.

Nevertheless he must hurry! The lamp will go out for lack of oil—like the lamp, the sick man is dying.

Yes, the bed is there—his own bed, surrounded by columns, his canopied bed closed by heavy curtains. Can this be a poor man's bed? With a shaking hand Doctor Trifulgas pulls the curtains apart and peers inside.

The dying man, his head barely above the sheets, is lying motionless as if hardly able to breathe. The doctor leans over him.

Doctor Trifulgas's cry is echoed outside by a sinister howl.

The dying man is not Vort Kartif: it is Doctor Trifulgas himself. He has been struck down by a congestion of the lungs; an apoplectic seizure has paralyzed half his body.

It is himself he has come to see, it is for himself that a hundred and twenty *fretzers* have been paid. Himself, who had refused to attend the dying man; himself, who is going to die.

Doctor Trifulgas thinks he is going mad. He feels utterly lost. His hands no longer obey him. With a supreme effort he manages to control himself.

What can he do? Diminish the blood pressure by bleeding the patient? Doctor Trifulgas is dead if he hesitates.

He opens his bag, takes out a lancet and pierces a vein in the dying man's arm. But the blood does not rise. He vigorously rubs the dying man's chest—he feels the beating of his own chest slowing down. He burns the dying man's feet with scorching stones—his own feet grow as cold as ice.

The man in the bed tries to sit up, struggles, and utters one final cry …

And Doctor Trifulgas, in spite of all the tricks which science has taught him, falls back dead in his own arms.

Next morning a body was found in Six-Four: that of Doctor Trifulgas. He was bathed in beer, placed in a wooden coffin and conducted with great pomp to Luktrop cemetery, where he now lies buried with so many others.

Translated from the French by Alberto Manguel.

The Legend of Sleepy Hollow

WASHINGTON IRVING

It was the very witching time of night that Ichabod, heavy-hearted and crestfallen, pursued his travel homeward, along the sides of the lofty hills which rise above Tarry Town, and which he had traversed so cheerily in the afternoon. The hour was as dismal as himself. Far below him, the Tappan Zee spread its dusky and indistinct waste of waters, with here and there the tall mast of a sloop, riding quietly at anchor under the land. In the dead hush of midnight, he could even hear the barking of the watch dog from the opposite shore of the Hudson; but it was so vague and faint as only to give an idea of his distance from this faithful companion of man. Now and then, too, the long-drawn crowing of a cock, accidentally awakened, would sound far, far off, from some farmhouse away among the hills—but it was like a dreaming sound in his ear. No signs of life occurred near him, but occasionally the melancholy chirp of a cricket, or perhaps the guttural twang of a bullfrog from a neighboring marsh, as if sleeping uncomfortably and turning suddenly in his bed.

All the stories of ghosts and goblins that he had heard in the afternoon now came crowding upon his recollection. The night grew darker and darker; the stars seemed to sink deeper in the sky, and driving clouds occasionally hid them from his sight. He had never felt so lonely and dismal. He was, moreover, approaching the very place where many of the scenes of the ghost stories had been laid. In the center of the road stood an enormous tulip-tree, which towered like a giant above all the other trees of the neighborhood and formed a kind of landmark. Its limbs were gnarled and fantastic, large enough to form trunks for ordinary trees, twisting down almost to the earth and rising again into the air. It was connected with the tragical story of the unfortunate André, who had been taken prisoner hard by, and was universally known by the name of Major André's tree. The common people regarded it with a mixture of respect and superstition, partly out of sympathy for the fate of its ill-starred namesake and partly from the tales of strange sights and doleful lamentations told concerning it.

As Ichabod approached this fearful tree, he began to whistle: he thought his whistle was answered—it was but a blast sweeping sharply through the dry branches. As he approached a little nearer, he thought he saw something white, hanging in the midst of the tree—he paused and ceased whistling; but on looking more narrowly, perceived that it was a place where the tree had been scathed by lightning, and the white wood laid bare. Suddenly he heard a groan—his teeth chattered and his knees smote against the saddle: it was but the rubbing of one huge bough upon another as they were swayed about by the breeze. He passed the tree in safety, but new perils lay before him.

About two hundred yards from the tree a small brook crossed the road and ran into a marshy and thickly-wooded glen, known by the name of Wiley's swamp. A few rough logs, laid side by side, served for a bridge over this stream. On that side of the road where the brook entered the wood, a group of oaks and chestnuts, matted thick with wild grapevines, threw a cavernous gloom over it. To pass this bridge was the severest trial. It was at this identical spot that the unfortunate André was captured, and under the covert of those chestnuts and vines were the sturdy yeomen concealed who surprised him. This has ever since been considered a haunted stream, and fearful are the feelings of the schoolboy who has to pass it alone after dark.

As he approached the stream his heart began to thump; he summoned up, however, all his resolution, gave his horse half a score of kicks in the ribs and attempted to dash briskly across the bridge. But instead of starting forward, the perverse old animal made a lateral movement, and ran broadside against the fence. Ichabod, whose fears increased with the delay, jerked the reins on

the other side, and kicked lustily with the contrary foot. It was all in vain: his steed started, it is true, but it was only to plunge to the opposite side of the road into a thicket of brambles and alder bushes. The schoolmaster now bestowed both whip and heel upon the starveling ribs of old Gunpowder, who dashed forward, snuffling and snorting, but came to a stand just by the bridge with a suddenness that had nearly sent his rider sprawling over his head. Just at this moment a plashy tramp by the side of the bridge caught the sensitive ear of Ichabod. In the dark shadow of the grove, on the margin of the brook, he beheld something huge, misshapen, black and towering. It stirred not, but seemed gathered up in the gloom, like some gigantic monster ready to spring upon the traveler.

The hair of the affrighted pedagogue rose upon his head with terror. What was to be done? To turn and fly was now too late, and besides, what chance was there of escaping ghost or goblin, if such it was, which could ride upon the wings of the wind? Summoning up, therefore, a show of courage, he demanded in stammering accents, "Who are you?" He received no reply. He repeated his demand in a still more agitated voice. Still there was no answer. Once more he cudgeled the sides of the inflexible Gunpowder, and, shutting his eyes, broke forth with involuntary fervor into a psalm tune. Just then the shadowy object of alarm put itself in motion, and, with a scramble and a bound, stood at once in the middle of the road. Though the night was dark and dismal, yet the form of the unknown might now in some degree be ascertained. He appeared to be a horseman of large dimensions, and mounted on a black horse of powerful frame. He made no offer of molestation or sociability, but kept aloof on one side of the road, jogging along on the blind side of old Gunpowder, who had now got over his fright and waywardness.

Ichabod, who had no relish for this strange midnight companion, and bethought himself of the adventure of Brom Bones with the Galloping Hessian, now quickened his steed, in hopes of leaving him behind. The stranger, however, quickened his horse to an equal pace. Ichabod pulled up and fell into a walk, thinking to lag behind. The other did the same. His heart began to sink within him; he endeavored to resume his psalm tune, but his parched tongue clove to the roof of his mouth, and he could not utter a stave. There was something in the moody and dogged silence of this pertinacious companion that was mysterious and appalling. It was soon fearfully accounted for. On mounting a rising ground, which brought the figure of his fellow-traveler in relief against the sky, gigantic in height, and muffled in a cloak, Ichabod was horror-struck, on perceiving that he was headless! But his horror was still more increased, on observing that the head, which should have rested on his shoulders, was carried before him on the pommel of the saddle. His terror rose to desperation; he rained a shower of kicks and blows upon Gunpowder, hoping, by a sudden movement, to give his companion the slip—but the specter started full jump with him. Away then they dashed, through thick and thin; stones flying and sparks flashing at every bound. Ichabod's flimsy garments fluttered in the air, as he stretched his long lank body away over his horse's head, in the eagerness of his flight.

They had now reached the road which turns off to Sleepy Hollow; but Gunpowder—who seemed possessed with a demon—instead of keeping up it, made an opposite turn, and plunged headlong down hill to the left. This road leads through a sandy hollow, shaded by trees for about a quarter of a mile, where it crosses the bridge famous in goblin story, and just beyond swells the green knoll on which stands the whitewashed church.

As yet the panic of the steed had given his unskillful rider an apparent advantage in the chase. But just as he had got halfway through the hollow, the girths of the saddle gave way, and he felt it slipping from under him. He seized it by the pommel and endeavored to hold it firm, but in vain, and had just time to save himself by clasping old Gunpowder round the neck, when the

saddle fell to the earth, and he heard it trampled underfoot by his pursuer. For a moment the terror of Hans Van Ripper's wrath passed across his mind—for it was his Sunday saddle. But this was no time for petty fears; the goblin was hard on his haunches, and (unskillful rider that he was!) he had much ado to maintain his seat; sometimes slipping on one side, sometimes on another, and sometimes jolted on the high ridge of his horse's back-bone, with a violence that he verily feared would cleave him asunder.

An opening in the trees now cheered him with the hopes that the church bridge was at hand. The wavering reflection of a silver star in the bosom of the brook told him that he was not mistaken. He saw the walls of the church dimly glaring under the trees beyond.

He recollected the place where Brom Bones's ghostly competitor had disappeared. "If I can but reach that bridge," thought Ichabod, "I am safe." Just then he heard the black steed panting and blowing close behind him; he even fancied that he felt his hot breath. Another convulsive kick in the ribs, and old Gunpowder sprang upon the bridge. He thundered over the resounding planks; he gained the opposite side; and now Ichabod cast a look behind to see if his pursuer should vanish, according to rule, in a flash of fire and brimstone. Just then he saw the goblin rising in his stirrups and in the very act of hurling his head at him. Ichabod endeavored to dodge the horrible missile, but too late. It encountered his cranium with a tremendous crash—he was tumbled headlong into the dust—and Gunpowder, the black steed, and the goblin rider passed by like a whirlwind.

The next morning the old horse was found without his saddle, and with the bridle under his feet, soberly cropping the grass at his master's gate. Ichabod did not make his appearance at breakfast—dinner hour came, but no Ichabod. The boys assembled at the schoolhouse, and strolled idly about the banks of the brook; but no schoolmaster. Hans Van Ripper now began to feel some uneasiness about the fate of poor Ichabod, and his saddle. An inquiry was set on foot, and after diligent investigation they came upon his traces. In one part of the road leading to the church was found the saddle trampled in the dirt; the tracks of horses' hoofs deeply dented in the road—and evidently at furious speed—were traced to the bridge, beyond which, on the bank of a broad part of the brook, where the water ran deep and black, was found the hat of the unfortunate Ichabod, and close beside it a shattered pumpkin.

The Cremation of Sam McGee

ROBERT SERVICE

There are strange things done in the midnight sun
By the men who moil for gold;
The Arctic trails have their secret tales
That would make your blood run cold;
The Northern Lights have seen queer sights,
But the queerest they ever did see
Was that night on the marge of Lake Lebarge
I cremated Sam McGee.

Now Sam McGee was from Tennessee, where the cotton
blooms and blows.
Why he left his home in the South to roam 'round the Pole,
God only knows.
He was always cold, but the land of gold seemed to hold him
like a spell;
Though he'd often say in his homely way that "he'd sooner
live in hell."

On a Christmas Day we were mushing our way over the
Dawson trail.
Talk of your cold! through the parka's fold it stabbed like a
driven nail.
If our eyes we'd close, then the lashes froze till sometimes we
couldn't see;
It wasn't much fun, but the only one to whimper was Sam McGee.

And that very night, as we lay packed tight in our robes beneath
the snow,
And the dogs were fed, and the stars o'erhead were dancing heel
and toe,
He turned to me, and "Cap," says he, "I'll cash in this trip, I guess;
And if I do, I'm asking that you won't refuse my last request."

Well, he seemed so low that I couldn't say no; then he says with
a sort of moan:
"It's the cursèd cold, and it's got right hold till I'm chilled clean
through to the bone.
Yet 'tain't being dead—it's my awful dread of the icy grave that pains;
So I want you to swear that, foul or fair, you'll cremate my
last remains."

A pal's last need is a thing to heed, so I swore I would not fail;
And we started on at the streak of dawn; but God! he looked
ghastly pale.
He crouched on the sleigh, and he raved all day of his home in
Tennessee;
And before nightfall a corpse was all that was left of Sam McGee.

There wasn't a breath in that land of death, and I hurried,
horror-driven,
With a corpse half hid that I couldn't get rid, because of a
promise given;
It was lashed to the sleigh, and it seemed to say: "You may tax
your brawn and brains,
But you promised true, and it's up to you to cremate those
last remains."

Now a promise made is a debt unpaid, and the trail has its own
stern code.
In the days to come, though my lips were dumb, in my heart
how I cursed that load.
In the long, long night, by the lone firelight, while the huskies,
round in a ring,
Howled out their woes to the homeless snows—O God! how I
loathed the thing.

And every day that quiet clay seemed to heavy and heavier grow;
And on I went, though the dogs were spent and the grub was getting low;
The trail was bad, and I felt half mad, but I swore I would not give in;
And I'd often sing to the hateful thing, and it hearkened with a grin.

Till I came to the marge of Lake Lebarge, and a derelict there lay;
It was jammed in the ice, but I saw in a trice it was called the "Alice May."
And I looked at it, and I thought a bit, and I looked at my frozen chum;
Then "Here," said I, with a sudden cry, "is my cre-ma-tor-eum."

Some planks I tore from the cabin floor, and I lit the boiler fire;
Some coal I found that was lying around, and I heaped the fuel higher;
The flames just soared, and the furnace roared—such a blaze you seldom see;
And I burrowed a hole in the glowing coal, and I stuffed in Sam McGee.

Then I made a hike, for I didn't like to hear him sizzle so;
And the heavens scowled, and the huskies howled, and the wind began to blow.
It was icy cold, but the hot sweat rolled down my cheeks, and I don't know why;
And the greasy smoke in an inky cloak went streaking down the sky.

I do not know how long in the snow I wrestled with grisly fear;
But the stars came out and they danced about ere again I ventured near;

I was sick with dread, but I bravely
said: "I'll just take a peep inside.
I guess he's cooked, and it's
time I looked"; ... then the
door I opened wide.

And there sat Sam, looking cool
and calm, in the heart of the
furnace roar;
And he wore a smile you could
see a mile, and he said:
"Please close that door.
It's fine in here, but I greatly
fear you'll let in the cold
and storm—
Since I left Plumtree, down in
Tennessee, it's the first time
I've been warm."

There are strange things done in the midnight sun
By the men who moil for gold;
The Arctic trails have their secret tales
That would make your blood run cold;
The Northern Lights have seen queer sights,
But the queerest they ever did see
Was that night on the marge of Lake Lebarge
I cremated Sam McGee.

The Hand

GUY DE MAUPASSANT

They had gathered in a circle around Monsieur Bermutier, the magistrate, who was expressing his opinion of the mysterious Saint-Cloud affair. For a whole month this inexplicable crime had been the talk of all Paris. Nobody could make head or tail of it.

Standing with his back to the fireplace, Monsieur Bermutier was talking away, marshaling evidence, discussing the various theories, but not reaching any conclusion.

Several women had got up and drawn nearer. They stood around him, their eyes fixed on the magistrate's clean-shaven lips which were uttering such solemn words. They shuddered and trembled, thrilled by that combination of fear and curiosity, that eager and insatiable love of being frightened, which haunts the minds of women, and torments them like a hunger.

There was a moment of silence. Then one of them, paler than the others, said: "It's terrifying! It seems like something supernatural. We shall never get to the bottom of it."

The magistrate turned toward her.

"Yes, madame. We probably never shall. But as for this word 'supernatural' that you've just used, it doesn't apply in this case. We are dealing with a crime that was so cleverly thought out—and so cleverly carried out—so thoroughly wrapped up in

mystery, that we cannot disentangle it from the baffling circumstances which surround it. But I once had to deal with a case which really *did* seem to have something supernatural about it. We had to abandon it, as a matter of fact, because there was simply no way of clearing it up."

Several of the womenfolk suddenly exclaimed, all at the same time: "Oh, *do* tell us about it!"

Monsieur Bermutier smiled the serious smile which befits an investigating magistrate, and went on:

"Now you mustn't imagine for a moment that I personally give a supernatural explanation to anything in this story. I believe only in natural causes. It would be much better if we simply used the word 'inexplicable' instead of the word 'supernatural' to describe what we do not understand. In any case, in the affair I am going to tell you about, it was the circumstances which led up to it which I found so fascinating. At any rate, here are the facts....

"At that time I was the investigating magistrate in Ajaccio, a little white town situated in a wonderful bay in Corsica, surrounded on all sides by high mountains.

"My particular job there was the investigation of vendettas. Some of them are sublime, ferocious, heroic, incredibly dramatic. In them you come across the finest stories of revenge imaginable, hatreds that have lasted for centuries—dying down for a while, but never extinguished—detestable trickery, murders amounting to massacre and almost becoming something they take a pride in. For two years I had heard talk of nothing else but the price of blood, and this terrible Corsican tradition which compels a man who has been wronged to take his revenge on the man who has wronged him, and on his descendants and relations. I have seen old men, children, cousins—all slaughtered. I used to have my mind filled with incidents of this kind.

"Now, one day I heard that an Englishman had just rented a little villa at the far end of the bay—and had taken a lease for several years. He had brought with him a French manservant he had taken into his service while passing through Marseilles.

"Soon everybody was taking an interest in this strange character who lived alone, and never went out, except to go hunting and fishing. He never spoke to anybody, never came into town, and every morning he would spend an hour or two in shooting practice, with pistol and rifle.

"Legends began to grow around him. It was claimed that he was a person of some importance who had fled his homeland for political reasons. Then people asserted that he was in hiding because he had committed some dreadful crime. They even supplied particularly horrible details.

"In my official capacity I tried to obtain some information about this man, but I found it impossible to learn anything—

except that he called himself Sir John Rowell.

"So I had to remain content with keeping a close watch on him—though, in fact, I had never received reports of anything suspicious concerning him.

"However, as the rumors grew worse and became more widespread, I made up my mind to see this stranger for myself, and started to make regular shooting expeditions in the neighborhood of his property.

"It was a long time before I had my opportunity, but at last it presented itself in the form of a partridge which I shot at and killed, right under the Englishman's nose, as it were. My dog brought the bird to me, but I took it straight away to Sir John Rowell and asked him to accept it, at the same time apologizing for having disturbed him with my shooting.

"He was a big man with red hair and a red beard, tall and broad-shouldered, a sort of calm, well-mannered giant. He had none of the so-called British stiffness, and he thanked me warmly for being so civil, speaking with a strong English accent. During the following month we chatted together five or six times.

"Then one evening, as I was passing his gate, I saw him smoking his pipe, sitting astride a chair in the garden. I greeted him, and he invited me into the garden to drink a glass of beer. I didn't need asking twice!

"He greeted me with all the meticulous courtesy typical of the English, was full of praise for France and Corsica and said, in very bad French, how fond he was of '*cette pays*' (this country) and '*cette rivage*' (this stretch of coast).

"Then I began to inquire about his past life and his plans for the future, asking my questions very tactfully and making a show of genuine interest in his affairs. He replied without any sign of embarrassment, and told me that he had traveled a good deal in Africa, India and America. He added, with a laugh, 'I've had plenty of adventures. I have indeed!'

"When I brought the conversation back to the subject of hunting he began to tell me all sorts of interesting things about the hunting of hippos, tigers, elephants—and even gorillas.

"'Those are all fearful brutes,' I said.

"'Oh, no!' he said, with a smile. 'The worst brute of all is man!' And he gave the hearty laugh of a big, genial Englishman, then he added: 'I've often hunted man, too.'

"Then he began to talk about guns and he invited me to come into the house and see the various types of guns he had.

"His drawing room was draped in black-black silk, embroidered with big golden flowers which were scattered over the somber material, gleaming like flames.

"'The silk is from Japan,' he said.

"But in the middle of the largest panel a strange object attracted my attention: it was black and stood out clearly against a square of red velvet. I went up to it. It was a hand, a human hand—not the hand of a skeleton, all white and clean, but a black, withered hand, with yellow nails, exposed muscles, and with traces of congealed blood, looking like dirt. The bones had been chopped off at about the middle of the forearm, as though they had been severed by an axe.

"An enormous iron chain was riveted and welded into the wrist of this filthy limb, and at the other end was attached to the wall by a ring strong enough to hold an elephant.

"I asked him: 'What's that?'

"The Englishman calmly replied: 'That's my worst enemy. It came from America. It was chopped off with a saber, skinned with a sharp bit of stone, and then dried in the sun for a week. And a damn good job it was, too!'

"I touched this human relic. It must have belonged to a man of gigantic size. The fingers, which were abnormally long, were held in place by enormous tendons which had fragments of skin still

clinging to them. The hand—flayed like this—was a frightening thing to see. You could not help thinking that it was the result of some barbaric act of vengeance.

"I remarked: 'This man must have been very strong.'

"The Englishman replied in a gentle voice: 'Oh, yes. But I was stronger than he was. I fixed that chain on his hand to prevent it from escaping.'

"I thought he must be joking, so I said: 'That chain won't be much use now. The hand won't run away!'

"Sir John Rowell then said in a very serious voice: 'It's *always* trying to get away. That chain is necessary.'

"I took a quick glance at his face, saying to myself: 'Is the fellow a madman—or a practical joker?'

"But his face remained inscrutable, with its placid, benevolent expression. So I changed the subject and began to admire his guns.

"I noticed, however, that three loaded revolvers had been placed on various items of furniture, as if this man were living in constant fear of being attacked.

"I made several more visits to his home, and then I stopped going there. We had become accustomed to his presence, and people now paid little attention to him.

"A whole year went by. Then, one morning, toward the end of November, my servant woke me with the news that Sir John Rowell had been murdered during the night.

"Half an hour later I was entering the Englishman's house along with the chief magistrate and the captain of the local police. Sir John's manservant, bewildered and in despair, was standing at the door in tears. At first I suspected this man—but he turned out to be innocent. We never did discover who the murderer was.

"When I entered Sir John's drawing room the first thing I saw was the corpse lying on its back in the middle of the room.

"His waistcoat had been torn; a sleeve of his jacket had been ripped away; everything pointed to the fact that a terrible struggle had taken place.

"The Englishman had been choked to death! His face was black and swollen—a terrifying sight—and the expression on it suggested that he had experienced the most appalling horror. There was something between his tightly clenched teeth, and in his neck, which was covered with blood, there were five puncture marks. They looked as though they had been made by fingers of iron.

"A doctor arrived. He spent a long time examining the imprints of the fingers in the flesh, and then came out with the strange remark: 'You'd think he'd been strangled by a skeleton!'

"A shudder ran down my spine, and immediately I looked at the place on the wall where I had previously seen the horrible flayed hand. It was no longer there. The broken chain was hanging down.

"Then I bent over the corpse. In his twisted mouth I found one of the fingers of the missing hand. It had been cut off—or rather sawn off—by the dead man's teeth, exactly at the second joint.

"We got on with our investigations. But we could discover nothing. No door or window had been forced, nothing had been broken into. The two guard dogs had not even wakened.

"Very briefly, this is the statement made by the servant. He said that for the past month his master had seemed very upset. He had received a lot of letters which he had burned as soon as they arrived. Often he had picked up a horsewhip and, in a display of anger which bordered on insanity, he had furiously beaten that withered hand, which had been riveted to the wall and which had, somehow or other, been removed at the very hour the crime was committed. Sir John used to go to bed very late, and he would carefully lock all the doors and windows. He always kept firearms within easy reach. Often, at night, he had been heard talking in a loud voice, as though he were quarreling with someone . . .

"On that particular night, as it happens, he had not made a sound, and it was only when he came to open the windows the next morning that the servant had found Sir John lying there, murdered. There was nobody this servant could think of as a suspect.

"I told the magistrates and police officers everything I knew about the dead man, and the most detailed inquiries were made over the whole island. Nothing was discovered.

"Now, one night, three months after the murder, I had a dreadful nightmare. I thought I saw the hand, the horrible hand, running like a scorpion, or a spider, all over the curtains and walls of my room. Three times I woke up, three times I fell asleep again, three times I saw that hideous human relic crawling rapidly around my bedroom, using its fingers as a creature uses its legs.

"In the morning this hand was brought to me. They had found it in the cemetery, lying on Sir John's grave. He had been buried on the island because they had not been able to trace his family. The hand had the index finger missing.

"Well, ladies. There's my story. That's all I know."

The women who had been listening were horrified, and looked pale and trembling. One of them exclaimed: "But that's not a proper ending! You haven't given us an explanation! We shall not be able to get to sleep tonight unless you tell us your opinion of what really happened."

The magistrate gave his austere smile: "Oh, ladies, I'm afraid I am going to deprive you of your nightmares! I simply think that the lawful owner of the hand was still alive, and that he came to get back his severed hand by using the one that remained. The only thing is, I just haven't been able to find out how he did it. It was obviously a sort of vendetta."

One of the women murmured: "No, that *can't* be the real explanation." And the magistrate, still smiling, finally remarked: "Well, I warned you my theory wouldn't satisfy you!"

The Golden Arm

TRADITIONAL ENGLISH FAIRY TALE

There was once a man who travelled the land all over in search of a wife. He saw young and old, rich and poor, pretty and plain, and could not meet with one to his mind. At last he found a woman, young, fair, and rich, who possessed a right arm of solid gold. He married her at once, and thought no man so fortunate as he was. They lived happily together, but, though he wished people to think otherwise, he was fonder of the golden arm than of all his wife's gifts besides.

At last she died. The husband put on the blackest black, and pulled the longest face at the funeral; but for all that he got up in the middle of the night, dug up the body, and cut off the golden arm. He hurried home to hide his treasure, and thought no one would know.

The following night he put the golden arm under his pillow, and was just falling asleep, when the ghost of his dead wife glided into the room. Stalking up to the bedside it drew the curtain, and looked at him reproachfully. Pretending not to be afraid, he spoke to the ghost, and said:

"What hast thou done with thy cheeks so red?"

"All withered and wasted away," replied the ghost, in a hollow tone.

"What hast thou done with thy red rosy lips?"

"All withered and wasted away."
"What hast thou done with thy golden hair?"
"All withered and wasted away."
"What hast thou done with thy *Golden Arm?*"
"THOU HAST IT!"

My Grandfather, Hendry Watty

SIR ARTHUR QUILLER-COUCH

'Tis the nicest miss in the world that I was born grandson of my own father's father, and not of another man altogether. Hendry Watty was the name of my grandfather that might have been; and he always maintained that to all intents and purposes he *was* my grandfather, and made me call him so—'twas such a narrow shave. I don't mind telling you about it. 'Tis a curious tale, too.

My grandfather, Hendry Watty, bet four gallons of eggy-hot that he would row out to the Shivering Grounds, all in the dead waste of the night, and haul a trammel there. To find the Shivering Grounds by night, you get the Gull Rock in a line with Tregamenna and pull out till you open the light on St. Anthony's Point. But everybody gives the place a wide berth because Archelaus Rowett's lugger foundered there one time, with six hands on board, and they say that at night you can hear the drowned men hailing their names. But my grandfather was the boldest man in Port Loe, and said he didn't care. So one Christmas Eve by daylight he and his mates went out and tilled the trammel, and then they came back

and spent the forepart of the evening over the eggy-hot, down to Oliver's tiddly-wink, to keep my grandfather's spirits up and also to show that the bet was made in earnest.

'Twas past eleven o'clock when they left Oliver's and walked down to the cove to see my grandfather off. He has told me since that he didn't feel afraid at all, but very friendly in mind, especially toward William John Dunn, who was walking on his right hand. This puzzled him at first, for as a rule he didn't think much of William John Dunn. But now he shook hands with him several times, and just as he was stepping into the boat he says, "You'll take care of Mary Polly while I'm away." Mary Polly Polsue was my grandfather's sweetheart at that time. But why he should have spoken as if he was bound on a long voyage he never could tell; he used to set it down to fate.

"I will," said William John Dunn; and then they gave a cheer and pushed my grandfather off, and he lit his pipe and away he rowed all into the dead waste of the night. He rowed and rowed, all in the dead waste of the night, and he got the Gull Rock in a line with Tregamenna windows, and still he was rowing, when to his great surprise he heard a voice calling:

"Hendry Watty! Hendry Watty!"

I told you my grandfather was the boldest man in Port Loe. But he dropped his two oars now and made the five signs of Penitence. For who could it be calling him out here in the dead waste and middle of the night?

"HENDRY WATTY! HENDRY WATTY! *Drop me a line."*

My grandfather kept his fishing-lines in a little skivet under the stern-sheets. But not a trace of bait had he on board. If he had, he was too much a-tremble to bait a hook.

"HENDRY WATTY! HENDRY WATTY! *Drop me a line, or I'll know why."*

My poor grandfather by this had picked up his oars again, and was rowing like mad to get quit of the neighborhood, when something or somebody gave three knocks—*thump, thump, thump!*—on the bottom of the boat, just as you would knock on a door. The third thump fetched Hendry Watty upright on his legs. He had no more heart for disobeying, but having bitten his pipe-stem in half by this time—his teeth chattered so—he baited his hook with the broken bit and flung it overboard, letting the line run out in the stern-notch. Not halfway had it run before he felt a long pull on it, like the sucking of a dogfish.

"Hendry Watty! Hendry Watty! Pull me in."

Hendry Watty pulled in hand over fist, and in came the lead sinker over the notch, and still the line was heavy; he pulled and he pulled, and next, all out of the dead waste of the night, came two white hands, like a washer-woman's, and gripped hold of the stern-board; and on the left of these two hands, on the little finger, was a silver ring, sunk very deep in the flesh. If this was bad, worse was the face that followed—a great white parboiled face, with the hair and whiskers all stuck with chips of wood and seaweed. And if this was bad for anybody, it was worse for my grandfather, who had known Archelaus Rowett before he was drowned out on the Shivering Grounds, six years before.

Archelaus Rowett climbed in over the stern, pulled the hook with the bit of pipe-stem out of his cheek, sat down in the stern-sheets, shook a small crayfish out of his whiskers, and said very coolly:

"If you should come across my wife—"

That was all my grandfather stayed to hear. At the sound of

Archelaus's voice he fetched a yell, jumped clean over the side of the boat and swam for dear life. He swam and swam, till by the bit of the moon he saw the Gull Rock close ahead. There were lashin's of rats on the Gull Rock, as he knew, but he was a good deal surprised at the way they were behaving; for they sat in a row at the water's edge and fished, with their tails let down into the sea for fishing-lines, and their eyes were like garnets burning as they looked at my grandfather over their shoulders.

"Hendry Watty! Hendry Watty! you can't land here—you're disturbing the pollack."

"Bejimbers! I wouldn' do that for the world," says my grandfather; so off he pushes and swims for the mainland. This was a long job, and 'twas as much as he could do to reach the Kibberick beach, where he fell on his face and hands among the stones, and there lay, taking breath.

The breath was hardly back in his body before he heard footsteps, and along the beach came a woman, and passed close by to him. He lay very quiet, and as she came near he saw 'twas Sarah Rowett, that used to be Archelaus's wife, but had married another man since. She was knitting as she went by, and did not seem to notice my grandfather; but he heard her say to herself, "The hour is come, and the man is come."

He had scarcely begun to wonder over this when he spied a ball of worsted yarn beside him that Sarah had dropped. 'Twas the ball she was knitting from, and a line of worsted stretched after her along the beach. Hendry Watty picked up the ball and followed the thread on tiptoe. In less than a minute he came near enough to watch what she was doing, and what she did was worth watching. First she gathered wreckwood and straw, and struck flint over touchwood and teened a fire. Then she unraveled her knitting, twisted her end of the yarn between finger and thumb—like a cobbler twisting a wax-end—and cast the end up toward the sky. It made Hendry Watty stare when the thread, instead of falling back

to the ground, remained hanging, just as if 'twas fastened to something up above; but it made him stare more when Sarah Rowett began to climb up it, and away up till nothing could be seen of her but her ankles dangling out of the dead waste and middle of the night.

"HENDRY WATTY! HENDRY WATTY!"

It wasn't Sarah calling, but a voice far away out to sea.

"HENDRY WATTY! HENDRY WATTY! *Send me a line!*"

My grandfather was wondering what to do, when Sarah speaks down very sharp to him, out of the dark:

"Hendry Watty! where's the rocket apparatus? Can't you hear the poor fellow asking for a line?"

"I do," says my grandfather, who was beginning to lose his temper; "and do you think, ma'am, that I carry a Boxer's rocket in my trousers pocket?"

"I think you have a ball of worsted in your hand," says she.

"Throw it as far as you can."

So my grandfather threw the ball out into the dead waste and middle of the night. He didn't see where it pitched, or how far it went.

"Right it is," says the woman aloft. "'Tis easy seen you're a hurler. But what shall us do for a cradle! Hendry Watty! Hendry Watty!"

"Ma'am to *you*," says my grandfather.

"If you've the common feelings of a gentleman, I'll ask you kindly to turn your back; I'm going to take off my stocking."

So my grandfather stared the other way very politely; and when he was told he might look again, he saw she had tied the stocking to the line and was running it out like a cradle into the dead waste of the night.

"Hendry Watty! Hendry Watty! look out below."

Before he could answer, plump! a man's leg came tumbling past his ear and scattered the ashes right and left.

"Hendry Watty! Hendry Watty! look out below!"

This time 'twas a great white arm and hand, with a silver ring sunk tight in the flesh of the little finger.

"Hendry Watty! Hendry Watty! warm them limbs!"

My grandfather picked them up and was warming them before the fire, when down came tumbling a great round head and bounced twice and lay in the firelight, staring up at him. And whose head was it but Archelaus Rowett's, that he'd run away from once already that night.

"Hendry Watty! Hendry Watty! look out below!"

This time 'twas another leg, and my grandfather was just about to lay hands on it, when the woman called down:

"Hendry Watty! catch it quick! It's my own leg I've thrown down by mistake."

The leg struck the ground and bounced high, and Hendry Watty made a leap after it.

And I reckon it's asleep he must have been; for what he caught was not Mrs. Rowett's leg, but the jib-boom of a deep-laden brigantine that was running him down in the dark. And as he sprang for it, his boat was crushed by the brigantine's forefoot and went down under his very boot-soles. At the same time he let out a yell, and two or three of the crew ran forward and hoisted him up to the bowsprit and in on deck, safe and sound.

But the brigantine happened to be outward-bound for the River Plate; so that, what with one thing and another, 'twas eleven good months before my grandfather landed again at Port Loe. And who should be the first man he sees standing above the cove but William John Dunn?

"I'm very glad to see you," says William John Dunn.

"Thank you kindly," answers my grandfather; "and how's Mary Polly?"

"Why, as for that," he says, "she took so much looking after, that I couldn't feel I was keeping her properly under my eye till I married her, last June month."

"You was always one to overdo things," said my grandfather.

"But if you was alive an' well, why didn' you drop us a line?"

Now when it came to talk about "dropping a line" my grandfather fairly lost his temper. So he struck William John Dunn on the nose—a thing he had never been known to do before—and William John Dunn hit him back, and the neighbors had to separate them. And next day, William John Dunn took out a summons against him.

Well, the case was tried before the magistrate: and my grandfather told his story from the beginning, quite straightforward, just as I've told it to you. And the magistrates decided that, taking one thing with another, he'd had a great deal of provocation, and fined him five shillings. And there the matter ended. But now you know the reason why I'm William John Dunn's grandson instead of Hendry Watty's.

Huw

GEOFFREY PALMER AND NOEL LLOYD

If you had asked me a couple of months ago whether or not I believed in ghosts I could not have given you a straight answer. I would probably have said, "Well, yes and no . . ." and gone on to explain that I could not answer one way or another because I had never actually seen such a thing, and though lots of odd things undoubtedly happen from time to time most of them surely have a rational explanation.

But that would have been a couple of months ago. Ask me the same question today and I would not hesitate to answer, "Yes, I *do* believe in ghosts, and what's more, I'm not a bit frightened of them." If you are wondering what happened to make me so definite I'd like to tell you all about it. I still find the whole thing very hard to accept, but I must accept it because it was real—it did happen.

It all began when my young brother Bryn invited me to spend a few days with him at Aberystwyth in Wales, where he was studying at the University. As I was between jobs my time was my own; and as a Welshman compelled to live in London the chance of spending some time in my home country was too good to miss. I accepted my brother's offer and decided to drive leisurely up through Shropshire and enter Wales by Snowdonia National Park instead of taking the quickest route.

The weather was good and I enjoyed the journey to the north-west. The Shropshire hills and valleys brought me into touch with

that special, unassuming loveliness that is one of the charming features of the English countryside. I even went out of my way to visit Clunton, Clunbury, Clungunford and Clun, just to discover whether they are, as Housman claims, "the quietest places under the sun." They were pretty quiet.

At last I headed west into Wales, keeping well away from the major roads, choosing instead any road that looked barely wide enough to take a car, hoping to reach Dolgellau, the friendly little town in a valley that is protected by Cader Idris. The trouble with driving aimlessly, enjoying the scenery and refusing to hurry, is that it is very easy to lose track of time—which is what happened to me. Daylight began to fade and the sky filled up with smoky clouds. There was a spatter of rain on the windscreen. The road was little more than a cart track and the country was very hilly. I thought I had better get on to a decent road as quickly as possible and head for Bala, leaving Dolgellau until the next day. At that point I realized I was running out of petrol.

It was quite dark by the time I had reached the main road and the petrol situation was serious. My map did not show any villages for several miles and I thought it quite likely that I would have to spend the night huddled up in the car in the middle of the Welsh mountains. Fortunately, this unpleasant vision faded when my lights picked out a solitary petrol pump by the side of a gray stone cottage. Of course, this little wayside petrol station was closed, but I was able to drag the owner away from his television set and persuade him to fill my tank.

I had only traveled a couple of miles farther when I saw the boy. By now the rain was very heavy and visibility was poor, but I saw him perfectly clearly as he stood by the side of the road, hands in pockets, looking toward the car. I pulled up and opened the on-side door.

"Missed your bus?" I called, taking it for granted that buses did run along this road. He didn't answer, but with a slight movement shook his head. He looked to be about thirteen or fourteen years old; he was tall and dressed in jeans and a black jacket buttoned up to his neck. His face was startling in its pallor.

"Do you want a lift?" I went on. "If so, jump in." This was no time to indulge in aimless conversation, and the boy's lack of interest rather irritated me. I pushed the door open a little more, wondering whether he was going to accept my offer, but he slid into the passenger seat without hesitation. I reached across him, closed the door and snapped the safety lock.

"What a night!" I said. "Have you missed your bus?" I asked him again—I could think of no other reason why a lad of his age should be standing in such a lonely spot on such a night.

He said nothing and I had to bite my lips to prevent myself making a sarcastic remark about the cat having bitten his tongue. I'll try once more, I thought. "Where are you going? Where can I drop you?"

This time he did answer me—in Welsh, and I mentally apologized to him for misunderstanding his silence. Perhaps he did not speak English very well, although clearly he understood it. "I'm afraid I know only a few words of Welsh," I said, "though I recognized the word 'trees'—something trees—can you translate?"

"Stricken," he answered in a husky adolescent's voice.

"Stricken Trees—that's an odd name. I can't remember anything like that on the map, either in English or Welsh. Is it a local name?"

"Yes," he said.

"And is it far?"

"No."

What marvelous dialogue, I thought, hoping that Stricken Trees was *very* near. I couldn't stand much more yes-ing and no-ing. Still, he was company of a sort, and talking to someone made a change from listening to the tires swishing over the wet road.

"Well, you'd better tell me when we get there," I said, "otherwise you'll find yourself in Bala." At that he twisted a little in his seat and turned to look at me. Ah, the first sign of life, I thought. Perhaps he's got a girl-friend in Bala and wouldn't mind being taken on there.

But the boy was showing agitation, not pleasure.

"What's the matter?" I asked.

"Don't go to Bala, mister," he said, with a sort of quivering urgency in his tone. "Not tonight...."

I could not help laughing at the intensity of his entreaty and my laugh was accompanied by a long roll of thunder. "Why not? There's nowhere to stay before Bala, and I am so tired and my joints ache so with the damp that I don't feel like driving the extra twenty miles or so to Dolgellau."

"Don't go to Bala, mister," he repeated.

"It's not as bad as that," I said jokingly. "Haven't you ever been there?"

"Not the last time," he said. "I never got there, you see."

I didn't see, but I let the subject drop. Frankly, I was beginning to feel a bit uneasy. I wondered if the boy was perhaps a bit simple—he was very unlike any fourteen-year-old I had ever met. "What's your name?" I asked, mainly for something to say.

"Huw," he replied. As he made no further contribution to the conversation I gave up and drove on in silence.

About ten minutes later, during which time I had, as I thought, been concentrating on the road, I remembered my passenger. "Huw, this place—Stricken Trees—are we anywhere near it?" My eyes were glued to the winding road and I could not tell whether he had heard me. "Huw!" I said, raising my voice. "Are you asleep? Are we anywhere near Stricken Trees?" Then the back of my neck tightened as though suddenly gripped in a vice, and without turning my head I knew.... I pulled the car into the side of the road to make absolutely sure. Huw was no longer sitting by my side.

I remember my feelings as if it had all taken place an hour ago. First, a quick stab of fear, then puzzlement as I tried the door and found it still locked, then an amused relief when I decided what had happened. Obviously Huw had told me where to stop, had got out and left me to continue alone. I had been guilty of falling asleep at the wheel—a constant fear of those who drive long distances alone. I had been driving by instinct… and could thank my guardian angel that the absence of any other vehicle had prevented an accident. "Let this be a lesson to you," I told myself. "You'd better stop at the next village for a rest and a snack." I let in the clutch and drove on, and within five minutes had reached a tiny village.

There was an inn among the dozen or so houses, and I parked the car and went in. An elderly lady sat behind the high counter, knitting. The small bar, hot and smoke-filled, was crowded with men puffing at pipes and talking in Welsh. But the landlady spoke to me in English with a musical lilt that seemed to embrace the whole scale. "Good evening, sir, *terr*ible weather, and what can I get you?" She slid off her stool and put down the knitting.

"A pint of bitter, please," I said. "And could you possibly make me a sandwich? I haven't eaten for hours."

The landlady disappeared into the back room and soon returned with the thickest, juiciest roast-beef sandwich I have ever eaten. It was a most welcome sight and I tucked into it eagerly. The other customers took little notice of me after their first casual glances, but Mrs. Cadwallader, as the landlady was called, and I got on famously. As it turned out I bought my milk from her brother's dairy at the corner of my road in London, and she had heard about my aged Auntie Blodwen who lived at the top of a hill in Flintshire and made lace that was known throughout North Wales. When I told her that I intended to spend the night in Bala she was delighted. "Beautiful town," she said, "and if you want a *love*ly place to stay, Morgan Llyfnant Arms is my brother-in-law. The

rooms overlook some fine gardens and on fine days you can see the lake and the linen is as crisp and clean as Snowdon's white cap!"

"The Llyfnant Arms it shall be," I promised. Talk of Bala had brought back vividly to my mind my strange passenger from Stricken Trees. Mrs. Cadwallader had turned to do something at the back of the bar and I raised my voice slightly. "By the way," I asked, "do you know a young lad from these parts named Huw?"

Every sound in the room suddenly faded. Mrs. Cadwallader, her back still turned to me, seemed to freeze. I could feel every eye swivel round and fix on the back of my head. I felt as though I had committed a crime—though what it was I had no idea. I blundered on. "And where is the place called Stricken Trees?"

When Mrs. Cadwallader turned round her eyes were full of sympathy, though not for me, as I soon realized, for she was looking past me into the room. "It's all right now, Mr. Griffiths," she said softly. "Don't you worry."

I shifted my position to see who Mr. Griffiths was and to guess why he shouldn't worry. From a solid group at the back there came forward a tiny wizened man with a skull-like face. Dark mournful eyes were the only living feature in it. When he spoke his voice was rich and deep, like an orator's. It was odd hearing it emerge from his spare frame.

"You have seen Huw tonight."

I didn't know whether he had made a statement or asked a question, but I felt like a schoolboy before a stern headmaster. "Yes, I gave him a lift about twelve miles back, to a place called Stricken Trees. To be honest, I don't remember dropping him."

"No, you wouldn't," Mr. Griffiths said, smiling grimly.

"I think I was overtired and dropped off to sleep for a few seconds."

"What did he say?"

"Not a lot," I replied. "He was a silent lad—at the awkward age, I suppose. Oh, he did tell me not to go to Bala tonight." I expected

smiles when I said that, but the only smile in the room was my own. There was another silent spell before Mr. Griffiths spoke again. "Then don't go to Bala tonight. . . ." He gave a curious sound like a strangled sob and with shoulders bowed he moved slowly across the room and went out into the night.

One man from the group got up as if to follow him, but another clutched his sleeve. "No, Dai, let him be. Nobody can help."

The others muttered agreement, so Dai sat down again. From that moment the atmosphere changed. No longer distant and clannish, the men crowded round me, asked me my name, where I came from, my profession, my taste in music and books, as if they were all trainee television interviewers, but never a word did they utter about Huw or Stricken Trees. I soon understood that they were deliberately avoiding those two topics, so I tried to probe the mystery. But every question was met by a chorus of false laughs.

"Huw? Only Ted Griffiths's boy."

"Worries about him, see?"

"Very close, that family."

"Have another drink?"

"No, thank you," I said. "Only one pint when I'm driving. But what have the Griffiths family got against Bala? I'm looking forward to seeing Morgan Llyfnant Arms."

More false laughter—even from Mrs. Cadwallader too. "Have another beer," was all I could get out of them. I had to get away. There was a mystery, but obviously I wasn't going to be let into the secret. I thanked the landlady, said good night to the men and promised I'd call again when I was in that part of the country. I was relieved to get back to my car, even though the rain was still tumbling down and the dark clouds were scurrying across the sky like crowds going to a football match.

Away from the village lights it was pitch-dark again. I tried to quell my uneasiness by humming "Men of Harlech," but before I had got to the end there was an ominous splutter from the engine. Please don't break down, I willed—not here; but the car stopped decisively, with a final spiteful chuckle. I was just about to get out and peer beneath the bonnet when the truth dawned on me. I was quite out of petrol! The needle registered an empty tank. It was impossible, but a fact.

Bristling with anger I went to the back of the car. The cap of the petrol tank was missing. Somebody had siphoned out all the six gallons I had bought at the wayside pump. I wished that I was not too old to burst into tears. As it was I had to clench my fists to contain my feelings. Then I caught a glimpse of someone standing by a wooden pole at the side of the road. It was Huw, peering at me, his white face caught in the headlights.

I dashed towards him. "Huw!" I cried. "What's going on? Who stole my petrol? Was it you or that strange father of yours?

Huw—where are you? Don't play tricks on me, for heaven's sake!"

But it was useless to keep on. He had disappeared. All that remained of Huw was a voice whispering in my ear, "Don't go to Bala tonight, mister. . . ."

I'm not going anywhere tonight, I thought despairingly, except to a makeshift bed in the back of the car. Idly I looked at the spot where Huw had been standing and noticed a painted board at the top of the wooden pole. Out of curiosity I got a torch from the car and shone it on to the board. I gave a gasp when the words on it were visible.

DAFYDD FARM 100 YARDS
BED & BREAKFAST
DAIRY PRODUCE

Well, if not a silver lining, this was at least a slightly less leaden one. I grabbed my case from the back seat, locked the car and trudged the hunched yards to Dafydd Farm, heedless of the rain and the ankle-deep mud.

Mrs. Jenkinson did not seem at all surprised to receive a visitor at such a late hour and welcomed me warmly. The farmhouse kitchen was scrubbed and spotless, and soon I was sitting down to a meal of ham and eggs that tasted better than anything the best four-star hotel could provide.

Mrs. Jenkinson hovered around me as I ate, making sure that I had everything I needed, and I found myself telling her the story of Huw, his father, my empty petrol tank and the strange behavior of the men in the inn. She nodded knowingly several times, and when she had put a huge dish of apple tart and clotted cream in front of me she sat down at the opposite side of the table.

"I dare say it all seems very mysterious to you, sir," she began, "but I think I can make things a bit clearer. Huw is a ghost. . . ." She uttered the words in a matter-of-fact way as though she might have been

saying, "Huw is a boy. . . ." She smiled at my start of surprise and went on, "The people in the village delude themselves that he only exists in the mind of his father, but he's a real ghost. I've seen him myself, and spoken to him, and I'm not one to imagine things, I can tell you."

"I'm sure you're not," I said. "Where does Stricken Trees come into the story?"

"That is where the Griffiths family lives. Years ago the trees outside their cottage were struck by lightning. Not a leaf has grown on them since, but the skeletons still stand there, bent and withered like rheumaticky old men. As for Huw—three years ago it happened—when the boy was thirteen. Ted Griffiths always maintained that he was delicate and wouldn't allow him to play out with the other boys, though when Huw got the chance to climb trees and kick a football it was clear that he was as strong as the rest of them. One day the traveling circus came to Bala. Huw wanted to go with his pals, but his father wouldn't hear of it. Said the night air might affect his chest and a lot of foolish things like that. I remember seeing the party set off in Wyn Evans's old bus, excited as only children can be at the thought of seeing clowns and tightrope walkers, lions and elephants. Huw waved them off and went back sadly to Stricken Trees. But he never arrived home because little Billy Price Top-shop had left his new bicycle leaning against his front wall, and as Huw passed by, looking both ways—it suddenly seemed as though the temptation was too much for him. He took the bike and rode off after the bus like the wind.

"If he had stopped to think he would have realized that there was no chance of getting to Bala in time for the circus as it's near enough twenty miles away and up and down hill all the way. But Huw *didn't* think. He just went on pedaling for all he was worth. He was about halfway to Bala when the tragedy happened—a chance in a thousand, it was. A huge boulder rolled down from the hill and knocked him off the bike into the path of a car coming toward him.

"He was hurt very badly. The people in the car were frantic with worry. They wrapped him up in a blanket, put him in the car and drove him to Stricken Trees as fast as they could—Huw was conscious at first and able to tell them where he lived. But by the time they had got there he was dead.

"His father nearly went out of his mind with grief and since then has shrunk away almost to nothing. Huw was the apple of his eye and he had little else to live for. Nowadays the only sign of life he shows is when he thinks Huw's ghost is about. Then he walks the roads seeking the boy, calling his name and asking forgiveness for not letting him go in the bus."

"Does Huw always warn people away from Bala, as he did me?" I asked.

"Now there's funny," said Mrs. Jenkinson. "I haven't heard of him doing that before. I wonder why he didn't want you to go there. . . ."

Even with so much to think about I slept well that night between sheets as Snowdon-white as those at Morgan Llyfnant Arms. Before I finally sank into sleep I wished I could give Huw a lift again. I would have been more understanding.

The next morning, after a wonderful breakfast, I set off early. Mr. Jenkinson, fortunately, was able to replace the missing petrol.

The aimless wanderings of the mountain sheep kept my mind on the serious business of driving, though I was able to marvel at the beauty of the towering mountains on one side of the road and the deep rich valleys on the other. When I saw the policeman ahead of me he seemed strangely out of place—directing traffic in that lonely spot surely wasn't necessary, I thought. He waved me to a halt and it was almost like being back in London.

"Sorry, sir," he said, when I poked my head out of the window. "I'm afraid you can't go any farther. Road to Bala's closed."

"But I must get there," I protested. "When will it be open again?"

"Couldn't say exactly, sir, but it'll be some time, I reckon."

"Has there been an accident?" For some reason my thoughts flew to Huw sprawled on the road with a car coming toward him.

"More an act of God, I'd say, sir."

"What *has* happened then?"

The policeman jerked a thumb behind him to the corner I had been approaching. "Landslide last night in all that rain. Near on half a mountain came down on the road and slid over into the valley. Thank your lucky stars you didn't start out any earlier yesterday and weren't anywhere near here last night, sir, or you'd never have got to Bala—*never*."

Huw, I thought, you can siphon the petrol out of my tank any time you like if your motive is always as good as it was last night. I reversed the car and drove back to find Stricken Trees. When Mr. Griffiths knew that Huw's ghost had saved my life his pride in his son would surely lighten his grief and give him the courage to face his loss.

So you see, that is why I believe in ghosts and why, if they are at all like Huw, there's no need to be afraid of them.

The Visitor

SEAN O'HUIGIN

one night
i woke up
when the rest
were asleep
and felt
something crawly
that started
to creep
up my arm
'neath the covers
i brushed it away
but it
didn't go
it wanted to stay
it creepy
crawled slowly
with long
hairy steps
it tickled
and whispered
and got to my neck
it sssssssed
and it husssshhhhhed
and it ssssshhhhhhhhhed
and it haaaaaaaahhhhed
it creeped 'cross my face
and it felt very odd
it crawled
'round my shoulders
and crept down
my back
then spidered away
and hid in the black

The King o' the Cats

JOSEPH JACOBS

In which Old Tom, the Sexton's big black cat, proves that he understands human speech. The spooky adventure begins when the Sexton returns home one night with a curious tale about nine black cats and a small black coffin marked with a gold coronet, which he has seen in the graveyard that very evening. Most curious was the message he was supposed to deliver. Who was Tom Tildrum?

One winter's evening the Sexton's wife was sitting by the fireside with her big black cat, Old Tom, on the other side, both half asleep and waiting for the master to come home. They waited and they waited, but still he didn't come, till at last he came rushing in, calling out, "Who's Tommy Tildrum?" in such a wild way that both his wife and his cat stared at him to know what was the matter.

"Why, what's the matter?" said his wife, "and why do you want to know who Tommy Tildrum is?"

"Oh, I've had such an adventure. I was digging away at old Mr. Fordyce's

grave when I suppose I must have dropped asleep, and only woke up by hearing a cat's *Miaou*."

"*Miaou!*" said Old Tom in answer.

"Yes, just like that! So I looked over the edge of the grave, and what do you think I saw?"

"Now, how can I tell?" said the Sexton's wife.

"Why, nine black cats all like our friend Tom here, all with a white spot on their chests. And what do you think they were carrying? Why, a small coffin covered with a black velvet pall, and on the pall was a small coronet all of gold, and at every third step they took they cried all together, *Miaou*—"

"*Miaou!*" said Old Tom again.

"Yes, just like that!" said the Sexton. "And as they came nearer and nearer to me I could see them more distinctly, because their eyes shone out with a sort of green light. Well, they all came toward me, eight of them carrying the coffin, and the biggest cat of all walking in front for all the world like—but look at our Tom, how he's looking at me. You'd think he knew all I was saying."

"Go on, go on," said his wife. "Never mind Old Tom."

"Well, as I was a-saying, they came toward me slowly and solemnly, and at every third step crying all together, *Miaou*—"

"Miaou!" said Old Tom again.

"Yes, just like that, till they came and stood right opposite Mr. Fordyce's grave, where I was, when they all stood still and looked straight at me. I did feel queer, that I did! But look at Old Tom; he's looking at me just like they did."

"Go on, go on," said his wife. "Never mind Old Tom."

"Where was I? Oh, they all stood still looking at me, when the one that wasn't carrying the coffin came forward and, staring straight at me, said to me—yes, I tell 'ee, *said* to me, with a squeaky voice, 'Tell Tom Tildrum that Tim Toldrum's dead,' and that's why I asked you if you knew who Tom Tildrum was, for how can I tell Tom Tildrum Tim Toldrum's dead if I don't know who Tom Tildrum is?"

"Look at Old Tom, look at Old Tom!" screamed his wife.

And well he might look, for Tom was swelling and Tom was staring, and at last Tom shrieked out, "What—old Tim dead! then I'm the King o' the Cats!" and rushed up the chimney and was nevermore seen.

Best Before

LAURIE CHANNER

Mackenzie pushed the leftovers and the limp celery aside to see all the way into the back of the refrigerator. The plastic yogurt tub was still there. Her dad hadn't seen it yet, or he would have thrown it out ages ago. It was blue-and-white and looked perfectly normal. But Mackenzie was afraid to open it. It had been there a long time. It would be really nasty inside. Green and fuzzy with mold, or maybe even *blue* and fuzzy. Mackenzie had even seen bright *purple* mold once. And the longer it stayed, the worse it would get.

She crouched there, looking way into the bottom shelf. The kitchen garbage was right nearby. She could just grab the container quickly and throw it straight in the bin without opening it.

Mackenzie reached in.

And it moved.

She yelped and yanked her arm back. The lid was bulging up. And up. But it stayed tight. So tight, it looked like it could pop off with just a little touch.

Mackenzie thought about the horrible, stinky air that was building up inside the yogurt tub. Yuck. She couldn't get rid of it without the smell making the whole house reek. Her dad would be mad for sure. Especially if the smell didn't go away for days, like skunk.

She put the other things back inside, making sure they hid, but didn't touch, the container. She shut the fridge door quickly and then froze, wondering if she'd slammed it hard enough to shake it into bursting. For a moment she stood, waiting to hear the "pop." It didn't come. Not yet.

Mackenzie ran out of the kitchen.

"Did you open it?" Jason asked. He was on his bike in her driveway.

Mackenzie sat down to put on her roller blades. "No way," she shook her head. "*I'm* not opening it." It was on a dare from Jason, her best friend, that she'd first pushed the yogurt tub to the back of the fridge. That was way before school let out for summer vacation. They were each going to let something go bad in their fridges. The winner would be the one who could make Roddy Blandings throw up. "The top goes like this now," she said, and traced the rounded shape in the air.

"Cool!" Jason said. "You're so lucky that you don't have a mom. My cheese was just getting really fuzzy when she found it and threw it away."

"My dad never cleans the fridge," Mackenzie said. But she was worried. Jason's mom had thrown his thing out, almost right after they'd started. Mackenzie had just forgotten about hers until yesterday, when Roddy had thrown up from being on the swings at the park. That reminded her. Now it was a week before school started again and the container had been in there all that time. By now it might make *her* throw up.

"Eeeew!" Jason said. "What if it goes off like a stink bomb? Blammo! Yucky stuff all over your kitchen. Then the Experts will have to come!"

Mackenzie didn't want that. They'd all heard about the Consumables Disposal Experts who had to be called when something went really bad in somebody's house, but none of the kids in the neighborhood had ever seen them. The Experts

were scary men in big, black rubbery coats with a mysterious truck that they dumped the bad stuff into. Roddy Blandings said that they put whoever was responsible for the stuff going bad into the truck as well, in a gunk tank with all the yuck they collected.

"They wouldn't come just for a yogurt container," Mackenzie said. She hoped it was true.

"You better throw it away now," Jason said.

"No way!" Mackenzie cried. "It might go blammo! when I touch it!"

"Then you better tell your dad," Jason said.

"He's at work," Mackenzie said. "I can't call him unless it's an emergency." Her dad was a landscaper and was at a different place every day.

"It *will* be an emergency when that thing goes blammo!" Jason laughed. "I'm getting out of here!" He hopped up on the pedals and started riding his bike toward the park.

Mackenzie looked anxiously back at the house, then tore off after him on her skates, yelling "Wait up!" the whole way.

It was lunchtime when they wheeled back to their street. Right away they knew something was wrong. They stopped at the corner and stared.

"Hey, that's your house," Jason said, like Mackenzie couldn't see for herself.

A big, black truck was parked right in front of Mackenzie's house. It was much bigger than Mackenzie's dad's pickup that usually sat there. Wide, yellow tape went all the way from the truck, up the front walk of her house and right in the door, which was open. The truck had a huge, concrete, canister-shaped thing on wheels towed along behind it. The thing had a lid like a sewer cover with a giant hinge.

"It's them, it's them!" Jason said. "And there's the gunk tank!"

Mackenzie got a very bad feeling in her stomach. The

Consumables Disposal Experts were in her house. That thing in the fridge must have gone *blammo!* after all. And her dad wasn't even home from work yet. "Let's go back to the park," she said. But she couldn't move.

Neighbors were standing on their lawns watching. The grown-ups were hanging on to their kids, not letting them go near the truck. There were rumors that just the smell coming out of the gunk tank would kill someone if they got too close. Mackenzie wondered if the smell from the yogurt tub would do the same thing. She sniffed the air a little bit, but didn't smell anything.

Two large men in big, black, buckled coats, big, buckled boots and shiny helmets came out of the front door of her house. They looked around, and their faces were hidden by scary bug-eyed gas masks. They wore air tanks like backpacks, and gloves, thick, rubbery ones that reached way up toward their elbows, swallowing the sleeves of their coats. All up and down the street, people took a step back when they came down the walk. Tiffany Wilkes ran from her mother and straight into her own house, banging the screen door as she ran inside.

The men took some equipment—heavy, long-handled tongs, and a big plastic bin and some other stuff—from the truck and carried it back inside.

Jason rode over to the nearest grown-up. The woman was standing in her driveway, pretending to wash her car, but watching just like everybody else. "Excuse me, ma'am," he said. "What's going on? That's her house," he pointed to Mackenzie, who wanted to hide.

The lady frowned at Mackenzie. "There must be something in there that's a risk to the neighborhood. It's very serious when the Experts have to come out. They're going to do an extraction."

"But we didn't call them!" Mackenzie said. "We aren't even home!" She wondered how they knew what she'd done.

"Oh, they can go right in if they need to," the lady said. "They're like the police that way." She gave Mackenzie a stern look. "And if nobody called them, it must be *very* serious indeed. You go over and tell them you live there. They'll want to see you."

Mackenzie didn't know that one little container could be a danger to the whole street. She also didn't like the sound of the word "extraction." It sounded like what they'd do to a ten-year-old who'd caused trouble. Extract her and put her in the gunk tank.

Mackenzie turned and skated away as fast as she could.

She went back to the park. It was empty. Every other kid was back on her street, watching the Experts.

Mackenzie swung on the swings, but it wasn't any fun. She stared at the ground and wondered if she could ever go home.

"Mackenzie!"

She looked up to see a man arriving at the park. A big man in a big, black coat and boots and helmet. He was coming straight for her, calling her name.

They knew! Mackenzie jumped off the swings to run away. But she forgot she was still in her roller blades and fell down hard in the grass. The man was running toward her now, in his black, scary, flapping rubber, like a bat, or a giant kid-eating bird. Mackenzie tried to run in her skates, but the grass was all bumpy and she stumbled again, twisting her ankle. She couldn't get up. The Expert's boots thumped closer behind her. She screamed and shut her eyes tight as he swooped down and grabbed her.

"Don't run, Mackenzie!"

Mackenzie howled and kicked. He scooped her up. "You have to come back with me," he said in a firm, deep voice.

She was going in the gunk tank, she knew it. "No! No!" she cried. She struggled as hard as she could. "Don't take me away!"

Mackenzie suddenly felt herself put down on the grass. The Expert squatted down and peered right into her face. "Mackenzie, just what do you think we're doing here?"

He wasn't wearing the bug mask any more, but under the helmet, he was scowling. Mackenzie was still frightened. "You took some stuff out of my fridge and now you're going to put me in the gunk tank," she said, the tears starting.

"We have a job to do to protect people," the Expert said. "There are a lot of nasty things around, nastier than they used to be. Things that cause sickness and disease. We can't let a germ get out and make your whole neighborhood sick. Now we need the number to reach your dad."

"My dad won't let you put me in the gunk tank!"

The Expert sat back and took off his fireman-type helmet. "Who told you that? You're not going in the tank!"

"Oh." For the first time, Mackenzie noticed that he had wavy brown hair, the same color as her dad's. "I'm not?"

The Expert reached out his big hand. Mackenzie ducked, but he just ruffled her hair. "Not if you help us do our jobs," he said and his eyes crinkled when he smiled.

Mackenzie stood on the porch of her house, while the Experts put their stuff away and rolled up the yellow tape. They were finished in her house now and they both had their black gear off. Underneath the coats they wore blue uniform shirts and pants that looked like the green ones Mackenzie's dad wore to work. They left the boots on. The second Expert had blond hair.

The neighborhood kids, including Jason, watched the Experts and then Mackenzie, like she was important now, too.

The Expert with the crinkly eyes went into the truck and came back out with something. It was a yogurt container with the brand name "Metro" in red on it. "Here," he said. "We cleaned it out. You can have it. The kid always gets to keep the container."

Mackenzie suddenly felt a very bad feeling. This wasn't her container. This other tub, it had been a new one her dad bought just last week. It had been in the front of the fridge. *Her* stuff was in a *blue*-and-white tub. A bulging blue-and-white tub. Maybe they hadn't seen it at the back of the bottom shelf. And hers didn't have just yogurt in it. She'd put bits of a whole bunch of different things that could go bad in. She'd even put in fertilizer from her dad's truck. She never told Jason that part, in case he thought it was cheating.

Mackenzie wanted to tell the men, but she couldn't. They might not be friendly any more if they knew she was growing something bad on purpose. But she also felt funny about not telling.

She could hear the blond one inside on the living room phone to her dad. "The checkout scanner at the Food Mart told us everyone who bought a certain kind of yogurt," he said. "Metro brand, 250 milliliters, plain, set style. It's a very, very bad batch. Contaminated at the dairy. Good thing no one had eaten any of it yet. I'm sorry, sir that we don't have time to give you the courtesy cleaning of the whole fridge, but we have a lot of stops to make. You might think about throwing that celery away, though."

Mackenzie slipped past him into the kitchen and stood in front of the fridge. It didn't look any different from before. But there was still something bad inside.

Through the open front door, she could hear doors slamming shut on the truck. Another few seconds and it would be too late to tell the Experts. Mackenzie still wasn't sure. Maybe if she looked again...

As she reached for the fridge handle, she heard a sudden, loud "pop." Mackenzie stopped with her hand still in midair.

The fridge began to shake.

Mackenzie screamed as the door flew open. A rotten-egg, sour-milk, garbagey smell rushed out. She screamed again as something large and slimy and turquoisey-green grew bigger on the bottom shelf. It pushed everything out in front of it. Jars of mustard and relish smashed onto the floor. It grew taller, too, changing shape all the way, knocking out the shelves above it. Milk and pop bottles burst as they hit the tiles. Stuff spattered everywhere and the thing in the fridge was still growing.

Mackenzie could only stand there, frozen to the spot. The horrible smell made her feel faint.

She didn't hear them coming, but suddenly the Experts were at the kitchen doorway. But then, the thing in the fridge leapt out at her.

It knocked her onto her back and plastered its hideous green self all over her. It was nearly as big as Mackenzie now, with vine-like limbs that it tried to wrap around her as she struggled. It was smothering her with its terrible, awful stink. She could hear the men shouting to each other.

"I'll pull it off, you get the tongs!"

She felt one of the Experts jump in to wrestle the creature away from her. It slid off and she squirmed away across the floor. It was plastered now across the Expert, the brown-haired one. She couldn't see his face under the writhing, smelly thing, just his hair. Mackenzie grabbed a bottle of disinfectant spray from the cupboard under the sink and started squirting. The creature flinched from the spray, but stayed on the man. His muffled yells were getting weaker.

The blond-haired Expert ran back into the kitchen with the

heavy black tongs and swung them down onto the green thing so hard Mackenzie worried about his partner underneath. Thin, white yogurt-blood spewed out in all directions. He smashed again and again. Mackenzie hid her face.

The yogurt-thing gave a hiss which became a gurgle. Suddenly everything was very quiet again.

Mackenzie opened her eyes. There was drippy yogurt goo all over the room, and the horrible green shapeless thing still wound around the Expert on the floor. "He's not moving," she said.

The blond Expert pried the creature off his partner. The man with the wavy brown hair lay very still.

"You hit him with the tongs!" Mackenzie cried.

"No," his partner said. "He suffocated under that *thing*." He knelt down. "I've never seen anything like it before." He shook his head in disbelief. "We handle food and germs, not *monsters*."

Mackenzie started to cry, right there on the floor. It was all her fault. "I'm sorry."

The Expert shook his head and looked very sad, too. "No, it's our fault. We should have checked the whole fridge when we still had our masks on. That would have saved him."

He sat on the floor and put an arm around Mackenzie and stared at his partner. "He'd be glad he saved *you*," he said.

Mackenzie couldn't stop crying.

It took a long time for things to be sorted out. Mackenzie's dad got home about the same time as the official people arrived to help the Expert put the yogurt creature in the gunk tank. The neighborhood watched, and Roddy Blandings threw up at the sight and smell of it. Then they took the dead Expert away.

A special crew cleaned up the fridge and the goo in the kitchen. When they were done, they offered her the blue-and-white yogurt tub, all scrubbed clean. Mackenzie didn't take it.

The Blackstairs Mountain

RUTH MANNING-SANDERS

Once upon a time a poor widow and her granddaughter lived in a tiny house on the top of a hill. From the windows of this tiny house you could see down into a green valley, and across the valley to a great mountain called the Blackstairs. Witches lived on the mountain. So every night, before they went to bed, the widow and her granddaughter did four things.

This is what they did: first, they loosed the band that worked the spinning wheel and laid it on the wheel-seat; second, they emptied the washing water into a channel that ran under the house door; third, they covered the burning turf on the hearth with ashes; fourth, they took the broom and pushed the handle of it through the bolt sockets of the house door, where the bolt itself had long ago rusted away. And, having done all that, they went to bed and slept soundly, knowing that the witches could not get in. Because the doing of these things formed a spell to keep the witches out.

But one day the widow and her granddaughter went to market, to sell the linen thread they had spun. It was a wild, wild

day, and a wilder night. Coming home, they took shelter from a storm of rain under some trees; and by the time the rain had eased off a bit, it was night; they missed their way in the dark, and didn't get home till very late.

When they did get home, they were so weary that their one thought was to get to bed; and they forgot all about the doing of those four things that they should have done to keep the witches out.

Well, they ate a sup and they drank a sup, and were making to go to their beds, when there came four loud bangs on the house door. They were making for the door then, to see who was knocking, when a voice screamed out of the night; and it was such an unholy scream that the widow and her granddaughter stood still in the middle of the kitchen and clutched each other in fear.

"Where are you, washing water?" screamed the voice.

And the washing water answered, "I am here in the tub."

"Where are you, spinning wheel band?" screamed the voice.

And the wheel band answered, "I am here, fast round the wheel, as if it were spinning."

"Broom, where are you?" screamed the voice.

And the broom answered, "I am here, with my handle in the dustpan."

"Turf coal, where are *you?*" screamed the voice.

And the burning turf answered, "I am here, blazing over the ashes."

Then—*bang, bang, bang, bang* at the door again, and a score of hideous voices howled, "Washing water, wheel band, broom, and turf coal, let us in!"

The door flew open: in rushed a great company of witches; and in their midst, leaping and yelling, was Old Nick himself, with his red horns and his green tail.

Pandemonium! Witches all round them, whirling about the kitchen, whooping, bawling, yelling with laughter. The grandmother fell down in a faint, and there was the terrified granddaughter

standing now in the midst of a throng of jeering, ill-favored faces and skinny waving arms, with her poor old grandmother lying like a dead thing at her feet.

Old Nick, with the red horns and the green tail, had seated himself on a stool by the fire. He had his hands to his nose, and he was pulling that nose in and out as if it were a trombone, and making the most hideous music with it. The witches began to dance to the music, kicking up their heels, leaping till their heads cracked against the ceiling, upsetting the chairs, the table, the pots and pans, the china and the crocks. *Smash*, went the widow's best china teapot; *smash, smash*, went cups and plates; *clitter, clatter, smash, smash*—everything was tumbling off the dresser. The very dresser itself reeled and swayed and toppled sideways against the window, and the window panes fell out with a crash.

"Oh what shall I do, what *shall* I do?" thought the poor terrified granddaughter. "Oh, if granny should die! If this goes on till cockcrow granny *will* die—she will never live to see another day! I must do something—but what *can* I do?"

Then an idea came to her. And if a good fairy didn't put that idea into the girl's head, then who did? The music that Old Nick was making with his nose became more and more hideous; the dance of the witches became more and more furious: screaming with laughter they leaped forth and back over the poor old grandmother, stretched on the floor in her faint. But they were taking no notice of the girl. So, holding her breath, and a step at a time, the girl sidled her way towards the house door. The door was still open. The girl slipped through it, and out into the night.

What did she do then? She screamed with all her might, rushed back into the kitchen, and shouted at the top of her voice, "Granny, Granny, come out! The Blackstairs Mountain and the sky above it is all on fire!"

Instantly the music stopped, and the dancing stopped. Old Nick made one leap through the window; the witches crowded after him, some through the door, some through the window. Out in the night rose a great and terrible cry, as with shrieks and lamentations the witches rose into the air and sped away through the darkness towards their home on the Blackstairs Mountain.

The shrieks and lamentations dwindled away into the distance, but the granddaughter hadn't wasted one moment in listening to them. Directly the last witch was out of the house, she seized up the broom and clapped the handle of it through the sockets where the door-bolt ought to be. Then she dragged the tub of washing water across the kitchen, and emptied the water into the channel under the house door. Then she loosed the band of the spinning wheel and laid it on the wheel-seat; and last, she raked the ashes in the hearth over the burning turf, till not one red ember could be seen. Having done all that, she ran to her granny and brought her to her senses by dashing cold water in her face.

The grandmother sat up. "Is all quiet at last?" she said.

"Yes, all is quiet," said the girl.

But no: from out in the night came a distant angry roaring; and the roaring grew nearer and nearer and louder and louder, as the witches came whirling back from their home, furious at the trick the girl had played on them.

The roar ended in sudden silence. Then—*tap, tap, tap, tap*: four quiet little knocks on the door.

"Washing water, let me in!" came a wheedling, whispering voice.

But the washing water answered, "I can't; I am spilled into the

channel under the door. I am trickling away round your feet, and my path is down to the valley."

"Spinning wheel band, *you* let me in!" came the wheedling voice.

But the wheel band answered, "I can't, I am lying loose on the wheel-seat."

"Broom, let me in!" whispered the wheedling voice.

"I can't," answered the broom. "I am put here to bolt the door."

"Turf coal, turf coal, open to me, open!" urged the whispering, wheedling voice.

And the hot turf answered, "I can't; my head is smothered with ashes."

Then came such a howling and cursing outside the door as made the widow and her granddaughter fall on their knees and cling together. But, howl and curse as they might, the witches could not get in. They whirled away through the night at last, back to their home on the Blackstairs Mountain.

The widow and her granddaughter had a job of it putting their house to rights. But you may be sure, after that night, never again did they go to their beds until they had loosed the spinning wheel band, emptied the washing water, piled ashes over the hot turf, and pushed the handle of the broom through the bolt sockets on the door.

Climax for a Ghost Story

I. A. IRELAND

HOW EERIE!" said the girl, advancing cautiously. "And what a heavy door!" She touched it as she spoke and it suddenly swung to with a click.

"Good Lord!" said the man. "I don't believe there's a handle inside. Why, you've locked us both in!"

"Not both of us. Only one of us," said the girl, and before his eyes she passed straight through the door and vanished.

Dracula's Guest

BRAM STOKER

When we started for our drive the sun was shining brightly on Munich, and the air was full of the joyousness of early summer. Just as we were about to depart, Herr Delbrück (the maître d'hôtel of the Quatre Saisons, where I was staying) came down, bareheaded, to the carriage and, after wishing me a pleasant drive, said to the coachman, still holding his hand on the handle of the carriage door:

"Remember you are back by nightfall. The sky looks bright but there is a shiver in the north wind that says there may be a sudden storm. But I am sure you will not be late." Here he smiled, and added, "for you know what night it is."

Johann answered with an emphatic, "Ja, mein Herr," and, touching his hat, drove off quickly. When we had cleared the town, I said, after signaling to him to stop:

"Tell me, Johann, what is tonight?"

He crossed himself as he answered laconically: "Walpurgis Nacht." Then he took out his watch, a great, old-fashioned German silver thing as big as a turnip, and looked at it, with his eyebrows gathered together and a little impatient shrug of his shoulders. I realized that this was his way of respectfully protesting against the unnecessary delay, and sank back in the carriage, merely motioning him to proceed. He started off rapidly, as if to make up for lost time. Every now and then the horses seemed to throw up their heads and

sniffed the air suspiciously. On such occasions I often looked round in alarm. The road was pretty bleak, for we were traversing a sort of high, wind-swept plateau. As we drove, I saw a road that looked but little used, and which seemed to dip through a little, winding valley. It looked so inviting that, even at the risk of offending him, I called Johann to stop—and when he had pulled up, I told him I would like to drive down that road. He made all sorts of excuses, and frequently crossed himself as he spoke. This somewhat piqued my curiosity, so I asked him various questions. He answered fencingly, and repeatedly looked at his watch in protest. Finally I said:

"Well, Johann, I want to go down this road. I shall not ask you to come unless you like, but tell me why you do not like to go, that is all I ask." For answer he seemed to throw himself off the box, so quickly did he reach the ground. Then he stretched out his hands appealingly to me, and implored me not to go. There was just enough of English mixed with the German for me to understand the drift of his talk. He seemed always just about to tell me something—the very idea of which evidently frightened him; but each time he pulled himself up, saying, as he crossed himself: "Walpurgis Nacht!"

I tried to argue with him, but it was difficult to argue with a man who did not know one's language. The advantage certainly rested with him, for although he began to speak in English, of a very crude and broken kind, he always got excited and broke into his native tongue—and every time he did so, he looked at his watch. Then the horses became restless and sniffed the air. At this he grew very pale, and, looking around in a frightened way, he suddenly jumped forward, took them by the bridles and led them on some twenty feet. I followed, and asked why he had done this. For answer he crossed himself, pointed to the spot we had left and drew his carriage in the direction of the other road, indicating a cross, and said, first in German, then in English: "Buried him—him what killed themselves."

I remembered the old custom of burying suicides at crossroads:

"Ah! I see, a suicide. How interesting!" But for the life of me I could not make out why the horses were frightened.

Whilst we were talking, we heard a sort of sound between a yelp and a bark. It was far away, but the horses got very restless, and it took Johann all his time to quiet them. He was pale, and said, "It sounds like a wolf—but yet there are no wolves here now."

"No?" I said, questioning him. "Isn't it long since the wolves were so near the city?"

"Long, long," he answered, "in the spring and summer; but with the snow the wolves have been here not so long."

Whilst he was petting the horses and trying to quiet them, dark clouds drifted rapidly across the sky. The sunshine passed away, and a breath of cold wind seemed to drift past us. It was only a breath, however, and more in the nature of a warning than a fact, for the sun came out brightly again. Johann looked under his lifted hand at the horizon and said:

"The storm of snow he comes before long time." Then he looked at his watch again, and, straightway holding his reins firmly—for the horses were still pawing the ground restlessly and shaking their heads—he climbed to his box as though the time had come for proceeding on our journey.

I felt a little obstinate and did not at once get into the carriage.

"Tell me," I said, "about this place where the road leads." And I pointed down.

Again he crossed himself and mumbled a prayer, before he answered, "It is unholy."

"What is unholy?" I inquired.

"The village."

"Then there is a village?"

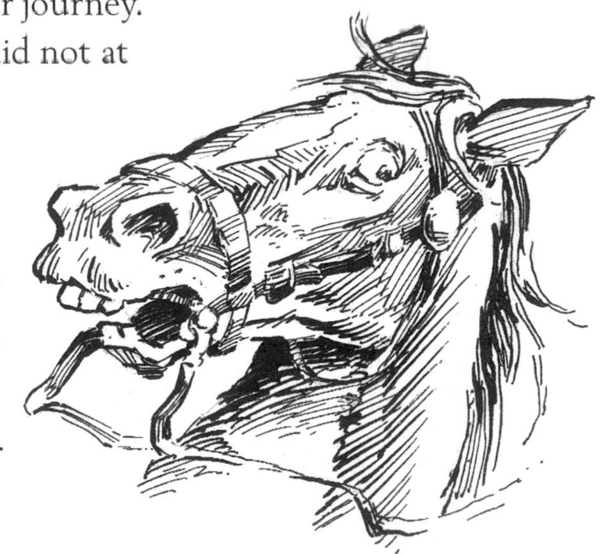

"No, no. No one lives there hundreds of years." My curiosity was piqued. "But you said there was a village."

"There was."

"Where is it now?"

Whereupon he burst out into a long story in German and English, so mixed up that I could not quite understand exactly what he said, but roughly I gathered that long ago, hundreds of years, men had died there and been buried in their graves. Sounds were heard under the clay, and when the graves were opened, men and women were found rosy with life, and their mouths red with blood. And so, in haste to save their lives (aye, and their souls!—and here he crossed himself) those who were left fled away to other places, where the living lived, and the dead were dead and not—not something. He was evidently afraid to speak the last words. As he proceeded with his narration, he grew more and more excited. It seemed as if his imagination had got hold of him, and he ended in a perfect paroxysm of fear—white-faced, perspiring, trembling and looking round him, as if expecting that some dreadful presence would manifest itself there in the bright sunshine on the open plain. Finally, in an agony of desperation, he cried:

"Walpurgis Nacht!" and pointed to the carriage for me to get in. All my English blood rose at this, and, standing back, I said:

"You are afraid, Johann—you are afraid. Go home; I shall return alone; the walk will do me good." The carriage door was open. I took from the seat my oak walking-stick—which I always carry on my holiday excursions—and closed the door, pointing back to Munich, and said, "Go home, Johann—Walpurgis Nacht doesn't concern Englishmen."

The horses were now more restive than ever, and Johann was trying to hold them in, while excitedly imploring me not to do anything so foolish. I pitied the poor fellow, he was deeply in earnest; but all the same I could not help laughing. His English

was quite gone now. In his anxiety he had forgotten that his only means of making me understand was to talk my language, so he jabbered away in his native German. It began to be a little tedious. After giving the direction, "Home!" I turned to go down the crossroad into the valley.

With a despairing gesture, Johann turned his horses toward Munich. I leaned on my stick and looked after him. He went slowly along the road for a while: then there came over the crest of the hill a man tall and thin. I could see so much in the distance. When he drew near the horses, they began to jump and kick about, then to scream with terror. Johann could not hold them in; they bolted down the road, running away madly. I watched them out of sight, then looked for the stranger, but I found that he, too, was gone.

With a light heart I turned down the side road through the deepening valley to which Johann had objected. There was not the slightest reason, that I could see, for his objection; and I daresay I tramped for a couple of hours without thinking of time or distance, and certainly without seeing a person or a house. So far as the place was concerned, it was desolation itself. But I did not notice this particularly till, on turning a bend in the road, I came upon a scattered fringe of wood; then I recognized that I had been impressed unconsciously by the desolation of the region through which I had passed.

I sat down to rest myself, and began to look around. It struck me that it was considerably colder than it had been at the commencement of my walk. A sort of sighing sound seemed to be around me, with, now and then, high overhead, a sort of muffled roar. Looking upward I noticed that great thick clouds were drifting rapidly across the sky from north to south at a great height. There were signs of coming storm in some lofty stratum of the air. I was a little chilly, and, thinking that it was the sitting still after the exercise of walking, I resumed my journey.

The ground I passed over was now much more picturesque. There were no striking objects that the eye might single out, but in all there was a charm of beauty. I took little heed of time, and it was only when the deepening twilight forced itself upon me that I began to think of how I should find my way home. The brightness of the day had gone. The air was cold, and the drifting of clouds high overhead was more marked. They were accompanied by a sort of faraway rushing sound, through which seemed to come at intervals that mysterious cry which the driver had said came from a wolf. For a while I hesitated. I had said I would see the deserted village, so on I went, and presently came on a wide stretch of open country, shut in by hills all around. Their sides were covered with trees which spread down to the plain, dotting, in clumps, the gentler slopes and hollows which showed here and there. I followed with my eye the winding of the road, and saw that it curved close to one of the densest of these clumps and was lost behind it.

As I looked, there came a cold shiver in the air, and the snow began to fall. I thought of the miles and miles of bleak country I had passed, and then hurried on to seek the shelter of the wood in front. Darker and darker grew the sky, and faster and heavier fell the snow, till the earth before and around me was a glistening white carpet the further edge of which was lost in misty vagueness. The road was here but crude, and when on the level its boundaries were not so marked as when it passed through the cuttings. In a little while I found that I must have strayed from it, for I missed underfoot the hard surface, and my feet sank deeper in the grass and moss. Then the wind grew stronger and blew with ever-increasing force, till I was fain to run before it. The air became icy-cold, and in spite of my exercise I began to suffer. The snow was now falling so thickly and whirling around me in such rapid eddies that I could hardly keep my eyes open. Every now and then the heavens were torn asunder by vivid lightning, and in the flashes I could see ahead of me a great mass of trees, chiefly yew and cypress all heavily coated with snow.

I was soon amongst the shelter of the trees, and there, in comparative silence, I could hear the rush of the wind high overhead. Presently the blackness of the storm had become merged in the darkness of the night. By and by the storm seemed to be passing away: it now only came in fierce puffs or blasts. At such moments the weird sound of the wolf appeared to be echoed by many similar sounds around me.

Now and again, through the black mass of drifting cloud, came a straggling ray of moonlight, which lit up the expanse and showed me that I was at the edge of a dense mass of cypress and yew trees. As the snow had ceased to fall, I walked out from the shelter and began to investigate more closely. It appeared to me that, amongst so many old foundations as I had passed, there might be still standing a house in which, though in ruins, I could find some sort of shelter for a while. As I skirted the edge of the copse, I found that a low wall encircled it, and following this I presently found an opening. Here the cypresses formed an alley leading up to a square mass of some kind of building. Just as I caught sight of this, however, the drifting clouds obscured the moon, and I passed up the path in darkness. The wind must have grown colder, for I felt myself shiver as I walked; but there was hope of shelter, and I groped my way blindly on.

I stopped, for there was a sudden stillness. The storm had passed;

and, perhaps in sympathy with nature's silence, my heart seemed to cease to beat. But this was only momentarily; for suddenly the moonlight broke through the clouds, showing me that I was in a graveyard, and that the square object before me was a great massive tomb of marble, as white as the snow that lay on and all around it. With the moonlight there came a fierce sigh of the storm, which appeared to resume its course with a long, low howl, as of many dogs or wolves. I was awed and shocked, and felt the cold perceptibly grow upon me till it seemed to grip me by the heart. Then while the flood of moonlight still fell on the marble tomb, the storm gave further evidence of renewing, as though it was returning on its track. Impelled by some sort of fascination, I approached the sepulchre to see what it was, and why such a thing stood alone in such a place. I walked around it, and read, over the Doric door, in German:

COUNTESS DOLINGEN OF GRATZ
IN STYRIA
SOUGHT AND FOUND DEATH
1801

On the top of the tomb, seemingly driven through the solid marble—for the structure was composed of a few vast blocks of stone—was a great iron spike or stake. On going to the back I saw, graven in Great Russian letters:

The dead travel fast.

There was something so weird and uncanny about the whole thing that it gave me a turn and made me feel quite faint. I began to wish, for the first time, that I had taken Johann's advice. Here a thought struck me, which came under almost mysterious circumstances and with a terrible shock. This was Walpurgis Night!

Walpurgis Night, when, according to the belief of millions of people, the devil was abroad—when the graves were opened and the dead came forth and walked. When all evil things of earth and air and water held revel. This very place the driver had specially shunned. This was the depopulated village of centuries ago. This was where the suicide lay; and this was the place where I was alone—unmanned, shivering with cold in a shroud of snow with a wild storm gathering again upon me! It took all my philosophy, all the religion I had been taught, all my courage, not to collapse in a paroxysm of fright.

And now a perfect tornado burst upon me. The ground shook as though thousands of horses thundered across it; and this time the storm bore on its icy wings, not snow, but great hailstones which drove with such violence that they might have come from the throngs of Balearic slingers—hailstones that beat down leaf and branch and made the shelter of the cypresses of no more avail than though their stems were standing-corn. At the first I had rushed to the nearest tree; but I was soon fain to leave it and seek the only spot that seemed to afford refuge, the deep Doric doorway of the marble tomb. There, crouching against the massive bronze door, I gained a certain amount of protection from the beating of the hailstones, for now they only drove against me as they ricocheted from the ground and the side of the marble.

As I leaned against the door, it moved slightly and opened inward. The shelter of even a tomb was welcome in that pitiless tempest, and I was about to enter it when there came a flash of forked lightning that lit up the whole expanse of the heavens. In the instant, as I am a living man, I saw, as my eyes were turned into the darkness of the tomb, a beautiful woman, with rounded cheeks and red lips, seemingly sleeping on a bier. As the thunder broke overhead, I was grasped as by the hand of a giant and hurled out into the storm. The whole thing was so sudden that, before I could realize the shock, moral as well as physical, I found the hailstones beating me down. At the same time I had a strange, dominating feeling that I was not alone. I looked toward the tomb. Just then there came another blinding flash, which seemed to strike the iron stake that surmounted the tomb and to pour through to the earth, blasting and crumbling the marble, as in a burst of flame. The dead woman rose for a moment of agony, while she was lapped in the flame, and her bitter scream of pain was drowned in the thundercrash. The last thing I heard was this mingling of dreadful sound, as again I was seized in the giant-grasp and dragged away, while the hailstones beat on me, and the air around seemed reverberant with the howling of wolves. The last sight that I remembered was a vague, white, moving mass, as if all the graves around me had sent out the phantoms of their sheeted-dead, and that they were closing in on me through the white cloudiness of the driving hail.

Gradually there came a sort of vague beginning of consciousness; then a sense of weariness that was dreadful. For a time I remembered nothing; but slowly my senses returned. My feet seemed positively racked with pain, yet I could not move them. They seemed to be numbed. There was an icy feeling at the back of my neck and all down my spine, and my ears, like my feet, were dead, yet in torment; but there was in my breast a sense of warmth which was, by comparison, delicious. It was as a nightmare—a physical nightmare, if

one may use such an expression; for some heavy weight on my chest made it difficult for me to breathe.

This period of semilethargy seemed to remain a long time, and as it faded away I must have slept or swooned. Then came a sort of loathing, like the first stage of seasickness, and a wild desire to be free from something—I knew not what. A vast stillness enveloped me, as though all the world were asleep or dead—only broken by the low panting as of some animal close to me. I felt a warm rasping at my throat, then came a consciousness of the awful truth, which chilled me to the heart and sent the blood surging up through my brain. Some great animal was lying on me and now licking my throat. I feared to stir, for some instinct of prudence bade me lie still; but the brute seemed to realise that there was now some change in me, for it raised its head. Through my eyelashes I saw above me the two great flaming eyes of a gigantic wolf. Its sharp white teeth gleamed in the gaping red mouth, and I could feel its hot breath fierce and acrid upon me.

For another spell of time I remembered no more. Then I became conscious of a low growl, followed by a yelp, renewed again and again. Then, seemingly very far away, I heard a "Holloa! holloa!" as of many voices calling in unison. Cautiously I raised my head and looked in the direction whence the sound came; but the cemetery blocked my view. The wolf still continued to yelp in a strange way, and a red glare began to move round the grove of cypresses, as though following the sound. As the voices drew closer, the wolf yelped faster and louder. I feared to make either sound or motion. Nearer came the red glow, over the white pall which stretched into the darkness around me. Then all at once from beyond the trees there came at a trot a troop of horsemen bearing torches. The wolf rose from my breast and made for the cemetery. I saw one of the horsemen (soldiers by their caps and their military cloaks) raise his carbine and take aim. A companion knocked up his arm, and I heard the ball whizz over my head. He had evidently taken my body for that of the wolf. Another sighted the animal as it slunk away, and a shot followed. Then, at a gallop, the troop rode forward—some toward me, others following the wolf as it disappeared amongst the snow-clad cypresses.

As they drew nearer I tried to move, but was powerless, although I could see and hear all that went on around me. Two or three of the soldiers jumped from their horses and knelt beside me. One of them raised my head and placed his hand over my heart.

"Good news, comrades!" he cried. "His heart still beats!"

Then some brandy was poured down my throat. It put vigor into me, and I was able to open my eyes fully and look around. Lights and shadows were moving among the trees, and I heard men call to one another. They drew together, uttering frightening exclamations, and the lights flashed as the others came pouring out of the cemetery pell-mell, like men possessed. When the further ones came close to us, those who were around me asked them eagerly:

"Well, have you found him?"

The reply rang out hurriedly:

"No! no! Come away quick—quick! This is no place to stay, and on this of all nights!"

"What was it?" was the question, asked in all manner of keys. The answer came variously and all indefinitely as though the men were moved by some common impulse to speak, yet were restrained by some common fear from giving their thoughts.

"It—it—indeed!" gibbered one, whose wits had plainly given out for the moment.

"A wolf—and yet not a wolf!" another put in shudderingly.

"No use trying for him without the sacred bullet," a third remarked in a more ordinary manner.

"Serve us right for coming out on this night! Truly we have earned our thousand marks!" were the ejaculations of a fourth.

"There was blood on the broken marble," another said after a

pause, "the lightning never brought that there. And for him—is he safe? Look at his throat! See, comrades, the wolf has been lying on him and keeping his blood warm."

The officer looked at my throat and replied:

"He is all right; the skin is not pierced. What does it all mean? We should never have found him but for the yelping of the wolf."

"What became of it?" asked the man who was holding up my head, and who seemed the least panic-stricken of the party, for his hands were steady and without tremor. On his sleeve was the chevron of a petty officer.

"It went to its home," answered the man, whose long face was pallid, and who actually shook with terror as he glanced around fearfully. "There are graves enough there in which it may lie. Come, comrades—come quickly! Let us leave this cursed spot."

The officer raised me to a sitting posture as he uttered a word of command; then several men placed me upon a horse. He sprang to the saddle behind me, took me in his arms, gave the word to advance; and, turning our faces away from the cypresses, we rode away in swift, military order.

As yet my tongue refused its office, and I was perforce silent. I must have fallen asleep; for the next thing I remembered was finding myself standing up, supported by a soldier on each side of me. It was almost broad daylight, and to the north a red streak of sunlight was reflected, like a path of blood, over the waste of snow. The officer was telling the men to say nothing of what they had seen, except that they found an English stranger, guarded by a large dog.

"Dog! that was no dog," cut in the man who had exhibited such fear. "I think I know a wolf when I see one."

The young officer answered calmly: "I said a dog."

"Dog!" reiterated the other ironically. It was evident that his courage was rising with the sun, and, pointing to me, he said, "Look at his throat. Is that the work of a dog, master?"

Instinctively I raised my hand to my throat, and as I touched it I cried out in pain. The men crowded round to look, some stooping down from their saddles; and again there came the calm voice of the young officer.

"A dog, as I said. If aught else were said we should only be laughed at."

I was then mounted behind a trooper, and we rode on into the suburbs of Munich. Here we came across a stray carriage, into which I was lifted, and it was driven off to the Quatre Saisons, the young officer accompanying me, whilst a trooper followed with his horse, and the others rode off to their barracks.

When we arrived, Herr Delbrück rushed so quickly down the steps to meet me that it was apparent he had been watching within. Taking me by both hands he solicitously led me in. The officer saluted me and was turning to withdraw, when I recognised his purpose, and insisted that he should come to my rooms. Over a glass of wine I warmly thanked him and his brave comrades for saving me. He replied simply that he was more than glad, and that Herr Delbrück had at the first taken steps to make all the searching party pleased; at which ambiguous utterance the maître d'hôtel smiled, while the officer pleaded duty and withdrew.

"But Herr Delbrück," I inquired, "how and why was it that the soldiers searched for me?"

He shrugged his shoulders, as if in deprecation of his own deed, as he replied:

"I was so fortunate as to obtain leave from the commander of the regiment in which I served, to ask for volunteers."

"But how did you know that I was lost?" I asked.

"The driver came hither with the remains of his carriage, which had been upset when the horses ran away."

"But surely you would not send a search-party of soldiers merely on this account."

"Oh, no!" he answered. "But even before the coachman arrived, I had this telegram from the Boyar whose guest you are," and he took from his pocket a telegram which he handed to me, and I read:

> Bistritz.
> Be careful of my guest—his safety is most precious to me. Should aught happen to him, or if he be missed, spare nothing to find him and ensure his safety. He is English and therefore adventurous. There are often dangers from snow and wolves and night. Lose not a moment if you suspect harm to him. I answer your zeal with my fortune. —*Dracula.*

As I held the telegram in my hand, the room seemed to whirl around me; and, if the attentive maître d'hôtel had not caught me, I think I should have fallen. There was something so strange in all this, something so weird and impossible to imagine, that there grew on me a sense of my being in some way the sport of opposite forces—the mere vague idea of which seemed in a way to paralyze me. I was certainly under some form of mysterious protection. From a distant country had come, in the very nick of time, a message that took me out of the danger of the snow-sleep and the jaws of the wolf.

A Change of Aunts

VIVIEN ALCOCK

Everyone knows the pond in Teppit's Wood is haunted. A young nursemaid once drowned herself there. She had done it early one evening, with the sun sinking in the red sky and the smoke from the burning house drifting through the trees.

They say she had slipped out to meet her sweetheart, and left the two little children alone, with the fire blazing behind its guard in the nursery grate. Burnt to cinders they were, the poor little ones, and the young nursemaid, mad with the guilt and grief of it, had done away with herself.

But she still can't rest, the tale goes; and at sunset, you'll see the smoke drifting through the trees, though a hundred years have passed since the big house burned down. Then, if you're wise, you'll run! For that's when the poor crazed ghost rises up, all wet from the dark pond, and goes seeking the dead children. Searching and searching all through the woods for the little children... *Take care she doesn't get you!*

Meg Thompson, who was eleven, thought perhaps she was too old to believe in ghosts. Her brother William believed in them, but he was only eight. Aunt Janet seemed to, but perhaps she was only pretending, just to keep William company, so that he need not feel ashamed.

Even in full daylight, Aunt Janet would hold their hands and run them past the pond, chanting the magic charm:

Lady of the little lake,
Come not nigh, for pity's sake!
Remember, when the sun is high,
We may safely pass you by.

And they would race up the hill through the trees, until they arrived home, laughing, breathless and safe.

They loved Aunt Janet, who had looked after them ever since their mother had died. Unfortunately, a neighbor's brother, come visiting from Australia, loved her too, and carried her back to Adelaide as his bride.

That was when Aunt Gertrude came. She was as different from Aunt Janet as a hawk from a dove. Thin and hard and sharp, she seemed to wear her bones outside her skin and her eyes on stalks. She could see dirty fingernails through pockets, smuggled bedtime cats through blankets, and broken mugs through two layers of newspaper and a dustbin lid.

"I'm up to all your tricks," she told them, with a smile like stretched elastic.

She only smiled when their father was in the room. There were many things she only did when he was there, such as calling them her dears, and giving them biscuits for their tea, and letting them watch television. Just as there were many things she only did when their father was out, such as feeding them on stale bread and marge, slapping and punching them, and locking them in the cellar as a punishment.

They did not mind being shut in the cellar. They played soldiers with the bottles of wine, or cricket with a lump of coal and a piece of wood. Or they sat on empty crates and planned vengeance on Aunt Gertrude.

"I'll get a gun and shoot her," William said. "I'll cut her up into little pieces with the carving knife and feed her to Tiddles."

"You'd only get sent to prison," Meg objected. "I'm going to write a letter to the Child Welfare and tell them about her, and they'll put *her* in prison."

"They won't believe you," William said, "any more than Dad does."

Meg was silent.

"Why doesn't Dad believe us?" William asked.

"Because she's always nicer to us when he's here. Because she doesn't hit us hard enough to leave bruises. Because she's told him we're liars." Meg hesitated, and then added slowly, "And because he doesn't *want* to believe us."

"Why not?"

"She's our last aunt. If she went, he wouldn't know what to do with us. He might have to send us away, and that would be worse."

William looked doubtful, but before he could say anything, there was the sound of a door shutting upstairs.

"She's back! Look sad, William," Meg whispered. They did not want Aunt Gertrude to find out they did not mind being locked in the cellar. She'd only think of another punishment. One that hurt.

"Meg," William whispered anxiously, "you haven't told her about the haunted pond, have you?"

Meg shook her head.

"She'd take me down there, I know she would. At sunset," William whispered, his eyes huge with fear. "At sunset, when it's dangerous to go."

"I won't let her," Meg said.

In September, their father had to go to Germany for a month on business. They both cried when he left, and this made Aunt Gertrude angry. As a punishment, she sent them to bed without supper, locking their rooms so that they could not sneak down in the night to steal food from the kitchen.

"I'm up to all your little tricks," she told them.

They were so hungry the next day that they were almost glad it was Wednesday. For every Wednesday, Aunt Gertrude took them to tea with a friend of hers, who lived in Eggleston Street, three miles away by road and no buses. Mrs. Brown was as square as Aunt Gertrude was angular, but otherwise seemed to be made of the same material. Granite. But at least they got sandwiches and cake there, and could shut their ears to the insults the two women aimed at them.

"The trouble I've had with them," Aunt Gertrude started off.

"I don't know what children are coming to, I'm sure," Mrs. Brown agreed. And they went on and on until at last it was time to go.

The walk back was all uphill. Usually Aunt Gertrude would

stride ahead, and shout at the children when they lagged behind. They never complained when their legs ached and blisters burst on their heels. They did not want Aunt Gertrude to find out about the shortcut through Teppit's Wood. But this Wednesday, as they were getting ready to go, Aunt Gertrude said that she was tired.

"Looking after these two wears me out. I must tell John he'll have to buy me a car. It's a long walk back up Eggleston Hill . . ."

"Up Eggleston Hill?" Mrs. Brown repeated, surprised. "Don't you take the shortcut through the wood?"

The children looked at each other in alarm.

"What shortcut?" Aunt Gertrude demanded. "I didn't know there was a shortcut. Nobody told me . . ." Her eyes looked round for someone to blame, and found the children: "Did you know about the shortcut?" she asked angrily.

"Of course they knew. Everyone knows," Mrs. Brown said. She looked at Meg and William and smiled nastily. "Don't tell me you're afraid to pass the haunted pond? I thought only babies were afraid of ghosts!" The sinking sun, shining through the window, flushed her face as if with wine. "Never mind," she said, her voice as falsely sweet as honey from a wasp, "I'm sure your dear Aunt Gertrude will cure you of such silly fancies."

William clutched hold of Meg's hand.

"I'm not going through the wood! I'm not! You can't make us! Not at sunset!"

Meg put her arms round him. She could hear Mrs. Brown telling Aunt Gertrude about the ghost of the young nursemaid, and Aunt Gertrude laughing scornfully.

"So you're frightened of ghosts, are you?" she said to the children, after they had left the house. "You'd let your poor aunt walk two unnecessary miles because of some stupid old wives' tale. Your poor aunt who works so hard while you spend all day playing! I'll soon see about that."

She grabbed them each by a wrist with her hard fingers and dragged them down the path into the woods. The trees closed round them in a dark, whispering crowd, seeming to murmur, "The sun is setting . . . keep away, keep away!"

William began to struggle and kick. Aunt Gertrude let go of Meg and hit William so hard that he was knocked right off the path. He fell into a deep drift of dead leaves, which rose up like brown butterflies and settled down on him as he lay whimpering.

Meg ran to comfort him. "You'll have a bruise," she whispered softly. "You'll have a big bruise to show Dad when he comes back."

He smiled through his tears.

"What's that? What are you two plotting?" Aunt Gertrude asked sharply. "Any more nonsense out of you, and there's plenty more where that came from. Well? Are you going to behave?"

She stood over them, tall and thin and hard as an iron lamppost, with the setting sun seeming to glow redly in her hateful eyes.

"Meg," William whispered, his arms round her neck, "I think she's a witch. Don't you? Meg, d'you think she's a witch?"

"No," Meg whispered back, more decidedly than she felt. "Come on, we'd better do what she says. Don't be frightened. I'll look after you, William."

So they walked down into the sighing woods. Their aunt marched behind them, throwing a long shadow that struck at their feet. William held tight to Meg's hand, and as soon as the dark pond came into sight, they began to chant under their breaths the words of the magic charm:

Lady of the little lake,
Come not nigh, for pity's sake!
Remember, when the sun is high . . .

"What are you two whispering about?" Aunt Gertrude demanded.

"Nothing," they answered.

For it was no good, the magic charm. It only worked in daylight, when the sun was up. Now the sun had fallen into the trees, and the sky was on fire.

"Look!" William whispered.

Between the trees, pale wisps of smoke came curling and creeping over the ground, like blind fingers searching . . .

"It's the smoke! Meg, it's the smoke!" William screamed.

Aunt Gertrude grabbed his shoulder and shook him.

"Stop that din! Making an exhibition of yourself! It's only mist rising from the water. Come, I'll show you." She started dragging William toward the pond. Meg grabbed him by the other arm, and for a moment they pulled him between them, like a cracker. Then Aunt Gertrude hit Meg hard on the ear, and Meg let go, putting her hands to her ringing head.

Aunt Gertrude forced William to the very edge of the dark pond.

"There! Look down, there's nothing there, is there, you stupid little coward? Answer me! There's nothing there, is there?"

She was looking at William as she spoke. She did not see what both the children saw. She did not see what rose out of the pond behind her.

It was something dark and wet, a figure of water and weeds. Green mud clung like flesh to its washed bones. A frog crouched like a pumping heart in its cage of ivory. Its crazed eyes, silver as the scales of fishes, glared down at Aunt Gertrude as she hit the terrified boy. It reached out . . .

Aunt Gertrude screamed.

William pulled away from her and ran. Blind with fear, he raced past Meg without seeing her, and disappeared into the trees.

Meg could not move. She crouched down on the damp, leafy ground and watched in terror. Dark water was torn from the pond in creamy tatters as the two figures struggled together, the screaming aunt and the other one, all water and weed and bone.

Its silver eyes glinting, it fastened its ivory fingers like combs into Aunt Gertrude's hair. Down, down they sank in a boil of bubbles.

"Meg! Meg!" William's voice called from among the trees, and Meg, as if released, leaped to her feet and ran after him, leaving Aunt Gertrude in the pond.

William had fallen over. His knee was bleeding, his bruised face wet.

"Come on, come on, hurry!" Meg said, catching hold of his hand and dragging him after her.

For there was someone following. Running through the trees behind them, twigs snapping, leaves crunching under invisible feet.

"Run, William, faster, faster!" Meg cried.

"I can't!"

"You must! Run, William, run!"

It was nearer now, and nearer, following fast, bounding in huge leaps over the rotting branches and white nests of toadstools.

"Faster!" Meg cried, looking fearfully over her shoulder at the shaking bushes, not seeing the twisted root that caught at her feet. She fell, bringing William down with her.

Aunt Gertrude burst through the bushes.

How strange she looked! She had run so fast that the clothes had dried on her body, and her cheeks were pink. Her hair, loosened from its tight knot, was tumbled and tangled about her head.

The children cowered away from her as she came up and knelt down beside them.

"Are you all right, my little dears?" she asked softly. (*Dears*?) "That was a nasty tumble! Why, you're shivering, Miss Margaret! And Master William, you've cut your poor knee." (*Miss*? *Master*?) "If you're a brave boy and don't cry, I'll give you a piggy-back home, and there'll be hot chocolate and cherry cake by the nursery fire."

They stared at her, trembling. The look in Aunt Gertrude's eyes was soft and kind. The smile on Aunt Gertrude's mouth was wide and

sweet. What was she up to? What cruel trick was she playing now?

They were silent as Aunt Gertrude carried William up the hill to their home. There, as good as her word, she gave them hot chocolate and cake, and sat them on the sofa while she bathed William's knee.

When she had finished, she stood up and gazed at the empty grate in the living room, while they watched her silently. Then she left the room. They sipped their hot chocolate, sitting side by side, listening. They could hear her going from room to room all over the house, as if looking for something.

"What's she up to?" William whispered.

"I don't know."

"Did you see it? Did you see it . . . in the pond?"

"Yes."

"What happened, Meg?"

"Aunt Gertrude fell in," Meg said, and shivered.

"Why is she so . . . so different?"

"I don't know."

"I wish Daddy were back," William said, and his lip quivered. Meg put her arm round him, and they were silent again, listening to the footsteps going round and round the house, slowly, uncertainly, as if Aunt Gertrude had lost her way.

There was no doubt that Aunt Gertrude was a changed woman since she had fallen into the pond. Perhaps the water had washed the nastiness out of her. The house had never been so bright and cheerful. Their meals had never been so delicious. She made them apple pie and cherry cake, and let them lick out the bowls. She played leap frog with them in the garden, and never minded running after the balls at cricket. She told them bedtime stories and kissed them good-night.

William started calling her Aunt Trudie, and would often hold her hand, taking her to see some treasure; a large snail with a whirligig shell, a stone with a hole right through the middle or a jay's feather. Meg followed them silently, watching and listening. Once, when William did not know she was behind them, she heard him say:

"Aunt Trudie, you mustn't call us Miss Margaret and Master William, you know."

"Should I not, Master William?"

"No. Just plain Meg and William."

"William, then."

"That's better. And when Daddy comes home on Saturday, you must call him John. Can you remember that?"

She smiled and nodded.

"Don't worry," he said. "I'll look after you, Aunt Trudie." Then he caught sight of Meg behind them and said quickly, "We're just playing a game. Go away, Meg! We don't want you!"

"Now, Mas...Now, William, that's no way to speak to your sister," Aunt Trudie said gently. "Of course we want her." She smiled at Meg. "We are going to see the kittens next door. Come with us, Meg."

Meg shook her head and walked back to the house. She went up to Aunt Gertrude's bedroom and looked round. It was bright and clean, and there were flowers on the dressing-table. There was no smell, no sense of Aunt Gertrude in it anywhere. It seemed like another person's room. Meg sat down on the bed and thought for a long time.

Aunt Trudie found her there, when she came in from the garden, flushed and laughing. She hesitated when she caught sight of Meg, then called over her shoulder, "Just a moment, William! Wait for me in the garden."

Then she shut the door and leaned against it, looking gravely and kindly at Meg.

"Will you be staying with us long?" Meg asked politely.

"As long as ever you want me to," was the answer.

There was a short silence. Then Meg jumped to her feet and put her arms round the woman.

"We don't want you to go, Aunt Trudie," she said. "We want you to stay with us forever."

It was three years before Meg ventured once more into Teppit's Wood. She went in broad daylight, when the sun was high. It was curiosity that took her there, down the winding path to the dark pond at the bottom. It was a warm day and birds were singing in the trees. The pond looked peaceful. There was frog-spawn in the brown water, leaves floated on the surface like little islands, and a water-boatman sculled across, leaving a silver wake behind him.

Meg stood a safe distance away and waited.

Bubbles began to disturb the quiet water. Small fish darted away and hid under the weeds. Now a scum of mud and filth rose slowly up from the bottom of the pond. It spread round a clump of frog-spawn, which shook and seemed to separate, and then reform into the shape of a hideous, scowling face.

As she watched, Meg thought she heard, faintly, a familiar voice.

"Meg! Get me out! Get me out this minute! She's stolen my body, that wretched servant-girl! Meg, if you bring her down here, I'll give you a penny. I'll give you chocolate biscuits every day. And roast beef! Just bring her down here and push her in! Meg, I'll never hit you again, I promise, I promise, promise ..."

"Goodbye, Aunt Gertrude," Meg said firmly, and left. That was the last time she ever walked in the woods round Teppit's pond.

The Strange Visitor

TRADITIONAL ENGLISH FAIRY TALE

A woman was sitting at her reel one night;
And still she sat, and still she reeled, and still she wished for company,

In came a pair of broad broad soles, and sat down at the fireside;
And still she sat, and still she reeled, and still she wished for company.

In came a pair of small small legs, and sat down on the broad broad soles;
And still she sat, and still she reeled, and still she wished for company.

In came a pair of thick thick knees, and sat down on the small small legs;
And still she sat, and still she reeled, and still she wished for company.

In came a pair of thin thin thighs, and sat down on the thick thick knees;
And still she sat, and still she reeled, and still she wished for company.

In came a pair of huge huge hips, and sat down on the thin thin thighs;
And still she sat, and still she reeled, and still she wished for company.

In came a wee wee waist, and sat down on the huge huge hips;
And still she sat, and still she reeled, and still she wished for company.

In came a pair of broad broad shoulders, and sat down on the
wee wee waist;
And still she sat, and still she reeled, and still she wished for company.

In came a pair of small small arms, and sat down on the broad
broad shoulders;
And still she sat, and still she reeled, and still she wished for company.

In came a pair of huge huge hands, and sat down on the small
small arms;
And still she sat, and still she reeled, and still she wished for company.

In came a small small neck, and sat down on the broad broad
shoulders;
And still she sat, and still she reeled, and still she wished for company.

In came a huge huge head, and sat down on the small small neck.

"How did you get such broad broad feet?" quoth the woman.
"Much tramping, much tramping" (*gruffly*).

"How did you get such small small legs?"
"*Aih-h-h!*—late—and *wee-e-e*—moul" (*whiningly*).

"How did you get such thick knees?"
"Much praying, much praying" (*piously*).

"How did you get such thin thin thighs?"
"Aih-h-h!—late—and wee-e-e—moul" (*whiningly*).

"How did you get such big big hips?"
"Much sitting, much sitting" (*gruffly*).

"How did you get such a wee wee waist?"
"Aih-h-h!—late—and wee-e-e—moul" (*whiningly*).

"How did you get such broad broad shoulders?"
"With carrying broom, with carrying broom" (*gruffly*).

"How did you get such small small arms?"
"Aih-h-h!—late—and wee-e-e—moul" (*whiningly*).

"How did you get such huge huge hands?"
"Threshing with an iron flail, threshing with an iron flail" (*gruffly*).

"How did you get such a small small neck?"
"Aih-h-h!—late—wee-e-e—moul" (*pitifully*).

"How did you get such a huge huge head?"
"Much knowledge, much knowledge" (*keenly*).

"What do you come for?"

"FOR YOU!" (*At the top of the voice, with a wave of the arm and a stamp of the feet.*)

The Monkey's Paw

W. W. JACOBS

I

Without, the night was cold and wet, but in the small parlor of Laburnum Villa the blinds were drawn and the fire burned brightly. Father and son were at chess; the former, who possessed ideas about the game involving radical changes, putting his king into such sharp and unnecessary perils that it even provoked comment from the white-haired old lady knitting placidly by the fire.

"Hark at the wind," said Mr. White, who, having seen a fatal mistake after it was too late, was amiably desirous of preventing his son from seeing it.

"I'm listening," said the latter, grimly surveying the board as he stretched out his hand. "Check."

"I should hardly think that he'd come tonight," said his father, with his hand poised over the board.

"Mate," replied the son.

"That's the worst of living so far out," bawled Mr. White, with sudden and unlooked-for violence. "Of all the beastly, slushy, out-of-the-way places to live in, this is the worst. Path's a bog, and the road's a torrent. I don't know what people are thinking about.

I suppose because only two houses in the road are let, they think it doesn't matter."

"Never mind, dear," said his wife soothingly; "perhaps you'll win the next one."

Mr. White looked up sharply, just in time to intercept a knowing glance between mother and son. The words died away on his lips, and he hid a guilty grin in his thin gray beard.

"There he is," said Herbert White, as the gate banged loudly and heavy footsteps came toward the door.

The old man rose with hospitable haste and, opening the door, was heard condoling with the new arrival. The new arrival also condoled with himself, so that Mrs. White said, "Tut, tut!" and coughed gently as her husband entered the room, followed by a tall, burly man, beady of eye and rubicund of visage.

"Sergeant-Major Morris," he said, introducing him.

The sergeant-major shook hands and, taking the proffered seat by the fire, watched contentedly while his host got out whisky and tumblers and stood a small copper kettle on the fire.

At the third glass his eyes got brighter, and he began to talk, the little family circle regarding with eager interest this visitor from distant parts, as he squared his broad shoulders in the chair and spoke of wild scenes and doughty deeds; of wars and plagues and strange peoples.

"Twenty-one years of it," said Mr. White, nodding at his wife and son. "When he went away he was a slip of a youth in the warehouse. Now look at him."

"He don't look to have taken much harm," said Mrs. White politely.

"I'd like to go to India myself," said the old man, "just to look round a bit, you know."

"Better where you are," said the sergeant-major, shaking his head. He put down the empty glass and, sighing softly, shook it again.

"I should like to see those old temples and fakirs and jugglers," said the old man. "What was that you started telling me the other day about a monkey's paw or something, Morris?"

"Nothing," said the soldier hastily. "Leastways nothing worth hearing."

"Monkey's paw?" said Mrs. White curiously.

"Well, it's just a bit of what you might call magic, perhaps," said the sergeant-major offhandedly.

His three listeners leaned forward eagerly. The visitor absent-mindedly put his empty glass to his lips and then set it down again. His host filled it for him.

"To look at," said the sergeant-major, fumbling in his pocket, "it's just an ordinary little paw, dried to a mummy."

He took something out of his pocket and proffered it. Mrs. White drew back with a grimace, but her son, taking it, examined it curiously.

"And what is there special about it?" inquired Mr. White as he took it from his son and, having examined it, placed it upon the table.

"It had a spell put on it by an old fakir," said the sergeant-major, a very holy man. "He wanted to show that fate ruled people's lives, and that those who interfered with it did so to their sorrow. He put a spell on it so that three separate men could each have three wishes from it."

His manner was so impressive that his hearers were conscious that their light laughter jarred somewhat.

"Well, why don't you have three, sir?" said Herbert White cleverly.

The soldier regarded him in the way that middle age is wont to regard presumptuous youth. "I have," he said quietly, and his blotchy face whitened.

"And did you really have the three wishes granted?" asked Mrs. White.

"I did," said the sergeant-major, and his glass tapped against his strong teeth.

"And has anybody else wished?" persisted the old lady.

"The first man had his three wishes. Yes," was the reply; "I don't know what the first two were, but the third was for death. That's how I got the paw."

His tones were so grave that a hush fell upon the group.

"If you've had your three wishes, it's no good to you now, then, Morris," said the old man at last. "What do you keep it for?"

The soldier shook his head. "Fancy, I suppose," he said slowly. "I did have some idea of selling it, but I don't think I will. It has caused enough mischief already. Besides, people won't buy. They think it's a fairy tale, some of them; and those who do think anything of it want to try it first and pay me afterward."

"If you could have another three wishes," said the old man, eyeing him keenly, "would you have them?"

"I don't know," said the other. "I don't know."

He took the paw and, dangling it between his forefinger and thumb, suddenly threw it upon the fire. White, with a slight cry, stooped down and snatched it off.

"Better let it burn," said the soldier solemnly.

"If you don't want it, Morris," said the other, "give it to me."

"I won't," said his friend doggedly. "I threw it on the fire. If you keep it, don't blame me for what happens. Pitch it on the fire again like a sensible man."

The other shook his head and examined his new possession closely. "How do you do it?" he inquired.

"Hold it up in your right hand and wish aloud," said the sergeant-major, "but I warn you of the consequences."

"Sounds like the *Arabian Nights*," said Mrs. White, as she rose and began to set the supper. "Don't you think you might wish for four pairs of hands for me."

Her husband drew the talisman from his pocket, and then all three burst into laughter as the sergeant-major, with a look of alarm on his face, caught him by the arm.

"If you must wish," he said gruffly, "wish for something sensible."

Mr. White dropped it back in his pocket and, placing chairs, motioned his friend to the table. In the business of supper the talisman was partly forgotten, and afterward the three sat listening in an enthralled fashion to a second instalment of the soldier's adventures in India.

"If the tale about the monkey's paw is not more truthful than those he has been telling us," said Herbert, as the door closed behind their guest, just in time to catch the last train, "we shan't make much out of it."

"Did you give him anything for it, Father?" inquired Mrs. White, regarding her husband closely.

"A trifle," said he, coloring slightly. "He didn't want it, but I made him take it. And he pressed me again to throw it away."

"Likely," said Herbert, with pretended horror. "Why, we're going to be rich, and famous, and happy. Wish to be an emperor,

Father, to begin with; then you can't be henpecked."

He darted round the table, pursued by the maligned Mrs. White armed with an antimacassar.

Mr. White took the paw from his pocket and eyed it dubiously. "I don't know what to wish for, and that's a fact," he said slowly. "It seems to me I've got all I want."

"If you only cleared the house, you'd be quite happy, wouldn't you!" said Herbert, with his hand on his shoulder. "Well, wish for two hundred pounds, then; that'll just do it."

His father, smiling shamefacedly at his own credulity, held up the talisman, as his son, with a solemn face, somewhat marred by a wink at his mother, sat down at the piano and struck a few impressive chords.

"I wish for two hundred pounds," said the old man distinctly.

A fine crash from the piano greeted the words, interrupted by a shuddering cry from the old man. His wife and son ran toward him.

"It moved," he cried, with a glance of disgust at the object as it lay on the floor. "As I wished, it twisted in my hand like a snake."

"Well, I don't see the money," said his son, as he picked it up and placed it on the table, "and I bet I never shall."

"It must have been your fancy, Father," said his wife, regarding him anxiously.

He shook his head. "Never mind, though; there's no harm done, but it gave me a shock all the same."

They sat down by the fire again while the two men finished their pipes. Outside, the wind was higher than ever, and the old man started nervously at the sound of a door banging upstairs. A silence unusual and depressing settled upon all three, which lasted until the old couple rose to retire for the night.

"I expect you'll find the cash tied up in a big bag in the middle

of your bed," said Herbert, as he bade them good night, "and something horrible squatting up on top of the wardrobe watching you as you pocket your ill-gotten gains."

He sat alone in the darkness, gazing at the dying fire, and seeing faces in it. The last face was so horrible and so simian that he gazed at it in amazement. It got so vivid that, with a little uneasy laugh, he felt on the table for a glass containing a little water to throw over it. His hand grasped the monkey's paw, and with a little shiver he wiped his hand on his coat and went up to bed.

II

In the brightness of the wintry sun next morning as it streamed over the breakfast table he laughed at his fears. There was an air of prosaic wholesomeness about the room which it had lacked on the previous night, and the dirty, shriveled little paw was pitched on the sideboard with a carelessness which betokened no great belief in its virtues.

"I suppose all old soldiers are the same," said Mrs. White. "The idea of our listening to such nonsense! How could wishes be granted in these days? And if they could, how could two hundred pounds hurt you, Father?"

"Might drop on his head from the sky," said the frivolous Herbert.

"Morris said the things happened so naturally," said his father, "that you might if you so wished attribute it to coincidence."

"Well, don't break into the money before I come back," said Herbert as he rose from the table. "I'm afraid it'll turn you into a mean, avaricious man, and we shall have to disown you."

His mother laughed and, following him to the door, watched him down the road; and returning to the breakfast table, she was very happy at the expense of her husband's credulity. All of which did not prevent her from scurrying to the door at the postman's knock, nor prevent her from referring somewhat shortly to retired sergeant-majors of bibulous habits when she found that the post brought a tailor's bill.

"Herbert will have some more of his funny remarks, I expect, when he comes home," she said, as they sat at dinner.

"I dare say," said Mr. White, pouring himself out some beer, "but for all that, the thing moved in my hand; that I'll swear to."

"You thought it did," said the old lady soothingly.

"I say it did," replied the other. "There was no thought about it; I had just—What's the matter?"

His wife made no reply. She was watching the mysterious movements of a man outside, who, peering in an undecided fashion at the house, appeared to be trying to make up his mind to enter. In mental connection with the two hundred pounds, she noticed that the stranger was well dressed and wore a silk hat of glossy newness. Three times he paused at the gate and then walked on again. The fourth time he stood with his hand upon it, then with sudden resolution flung it open and walked up the path. Mrs White at the same moment placed her hands behind her, and hurriedly unfastening the strings of her apron, put that useful article of apparel beneath the cushion of her chair.

She brought the stranger, who seemed ill at ease, into the room. He gazed at her furtively and listened in a preoccupied fashion as the old lady apologized for the appearance of the room, and her husband's coat, a garment which he usually reserved for the garden. She then waited as patiently as her sex would permit for him to broach his business, but he was at first strangely silent.

"I—was asked to call," he said at last, and stooped and picked a piece of cotton from his trousers. "I come from Maw and Meggins."

The old lady started. "Is anything the matter?" she asked breathlessly. "Has anything happened to Herbert? What is it? What is it?"

Her husband interposed. "There, there, Mother," he said hastily. "Sit down, and don't jump to conclusions. You've not brought bad news, I'm sure, sir," and he eyed the other wistfully.

"I'm sorry—" began the visitor.

"Is he hurt?" demanded the mother wildly.

The visitor bowed in assent. "Badly hurt," he said quietly, "but he is not in any pain."

"Oh, thank God!" said the old woman, clasping her hands. "Thank God for that! Thank—"

She broke off suddenly as the sinister meaning of the assurance dawned upon her and she saw the awful confirmation of her fears in the other's averted face. She caught her breath and, turning to her slower-witted husband, laid her trembling old hand upon his. There was a long silence.

"He was caught in the machinery," said the visitor at length in a low voice.

"Caught in the machinery," repeated Mr. White, in a dazed fashion, "yes."

He sat staring blankly out of the window and, taking his wife's hand between his own, pressed it as he had been wont to do in their old courting days nearly forty years before.

"He was the only one left to us," he said, turning gently to the visitor. "It is hard."

The other coughed and, rising, walked slowly to the window. "The firm wished me to convey their sincere sympathy with you in your great loss," he said, without looking round. "I beg that you will understand I am only their servant and merely obeying orders."

There was no reply; the old woman's face was white, her eyes staring and her breath inaudible; on the husband's face was a look such as his friend the sergeant might have carried into his first action.

"I was to say that Maw and Meggins disclaim all responsibility," continued the other. "They admit no liability at all, but in consideration of your son's services, they wish to present you with a certain sum as compensation."

Mr. White dropped his wife's hand and, rising to his feet, gazed with a look of horror at his visitor. His dry lips shaped the words, "How much?"

"Two hundred pounds," was the answer.

Unconscious of his wife's shriek, the old man smiled faintly, put out his hands like a sightless man, and dropped, a senseless heap, to the floor.

III

In the huge new cemetery, some two miles distant, the old people buried their dead and came back to the house steeped in shadow and silence. It was all over so quickly that at first they could hardly realize it, and remained in a state of expectation as though of something else to happen—something else which was to lighten this load, too heavy for old hearts to bear.

But the days passed, and expectation gave place to resignation—the hopeless resignation of the old, sometimes miscalled apathy. Sometimes they hardly exchanged a word, for now they had nothing to talk about, and their days were long to weariness.

It was about a week after that the old man, waking suddenly in the night, stretched out his hand and found himself alone. The room was in darkness, and the sound of subdued weeping came from the window. He raised himself in bed and listened.

"Come back," he said tenderly. "You will be cold."

"It is colder for my son," said the old woman, and wept afresh.

The sound of her sobs died away on his ears. The bed was warm, and his eyes heavy with sleep. He dozed fitfully and then slept until a sudden wild cry from his wife awoke him with a start.

"*The paw!*" she cried wildly. "The monkey's paw!"

He started up in alarm. "Where? Where is it? What's the matter?"

She came stumbling across the room toward him. "I want it," she said quietly. "You've not destroyed it?"

"It's in the parlor, on the bracket," he replied, marveling. "Why?"

She cried and laughed together and, bending over, kissed his cheek.

"I only just thought of it," she said hysterically. "Why didn't I think of it before? Why didn't *you* think of it?"

"Think of what?" he questioned.

"The other two wishes," she replied rapidly. "We've only had one."

"Was not that enough?" he demanded fiercely.

"No," she cried triumphantly; "we'll have one more. Go down and get it quickly, and wish our boy alive again."

The man sat up in bed and flung the bedclothes from his quaking limbs. "Good God, you are mad!" he cried, aghast.

"Get it," she panted. "Get it quickly and wish—Oh, my boy, my boy!"

Her husband struck a match and lit the candle. "Get back to bed," he said unsteadily. "You don't know what you are saying."

"We had the first wish granted," said the old woman feverishly, "why not the second?"

"A coincidence," stammered the old man.

"Go and get it and wish," cried his wife, quivering with excitement.

The old man turned and regarded her, and his voice shook. "He has been dead ten days, and besides he—I would not tell you else, but—I could only recognize him by his clothing. If he was too terrible for you to see then, how now?"

"Bring him back," cried the old woman, and dragged him toward the door. "Do you think I fear the child I have nursed?"

He went down in the darkness and felt his way to the parlor, and then to the mantelpiece. The talisman was in its place, and a horrible fear that the unspoken wish might bring his mutilated son before him ere he could escape from the room seized upon him, and he caught his breath as he found that he had lost the direction of the door. His brow cold with sweat, he felt his way round the table and groped along the wall until he found himself in the small passage with the unwholesome thing in his hand.

Even his wife's face seemed changed as he entered the room. It was white and expectant, and to his fears seemed to have an unnatural look upon it. He was afraid of her.

"*Wish!*" she cried in a strong voice.

"It is foolish and wicked," he faltered.

"*Wish!*" repeated his wife.

He raised his hand. "I wish my son alive again."

The talisman fell to the floor, and he regarded it fearfully. Then he sank trembling into a chair as the old woman, with burning eyes, walked to the window and raised the blind.

He sat until he was chilled with the cold, glancing occasionally at the figure of the old woman peering through the window. The candle end, which had burned below the rim of the china candlestick, was throwing pulsating shadows on the ceiling and walls, until, with a flicker larger than the rest, it expired. The old man, with an unspeakable sense of relief at the failure of the talisman, crept back to his bed, and a minute or two afterward the old woman came silently and apathetically beside him.

Neither spoke, but lay silently listening to the ticking of the clock. A stair creaked, and a squeaky mouse scurried noisily through the wall. The darkness was oppressive, and after lying for some time screwing up his courage, he took the box of matches, and striking one, went downstairs for a candle.

At the foot of the stairs the match went out, and he paused to strike another; and at the same moment a knock, so quiet and stealthy as to be scarcely audible, sounded on the front door.

The matches fell from his hand and spilled in the passage. He stood motionless, his breath suspended until the knock was repeated. Then he turned and fled swiftly back to his room, and closed the door behind him. A third knock sounded through the house.

"*What's that?*" cried the old woman, starting up.

"A rat," said the old man in shaking tones—"a rat. It passed me on the stairs."

His wife sat up in bed listening. A loud knock resounded through the house.

"It's Herbert!" she screamed. "It's Herbert!"

She ran to the door, but her husband was before her, and catching her by the arm, held her tightly.

"What are you going to do?" he whispered hoarsely.

"It's my boy; it's Herbert!" she cried, struggling mechanically. "I forgot it was two miles away. What are you holding me for? Let go. I must open the door."

"For God's sake don't let it in," cried the old man, trembling.

"You're afraid of your own son," she cried, struggling. "Let me go. I'm coming Herbert; I'm coming."

There was another knock, and another. The old woman with

a sudden wrench broke free and ran from the room. Her husband followed to the landing and called after her appealingly as she hurried downstairs. He heard the chain rattle back and the bottom bolt drawn slowly and stiffly from the socket. Then the old woman's voice, strained and panting.

"The bolt," she cried loudly. "Come down. I can't reach it."

But her husband was on his hands and knees groping wildly on the floor in search of the paw. If he could only find it before the thing outside got in. A perfect fusillade of knocks reverberated through the house, and he heard the scraping of a chair as his wife put it down in the passage against the door. He heard the creaking of the bolt as it came slowly back, and at the same moment he found the monkey's paw, and frantically breathed his third and last wish.

The knocking ceased suddenly, although the echoes of it were still in the house. He heard the chair drawn back, and the door opened. A cold wind rushed up the staircase, and a long loud wail of disappointment and misery from his wife gave him courage to run down to her side, and then to the gate beyond. The street lamp flickering opposite shone on a quiet and deserted road.

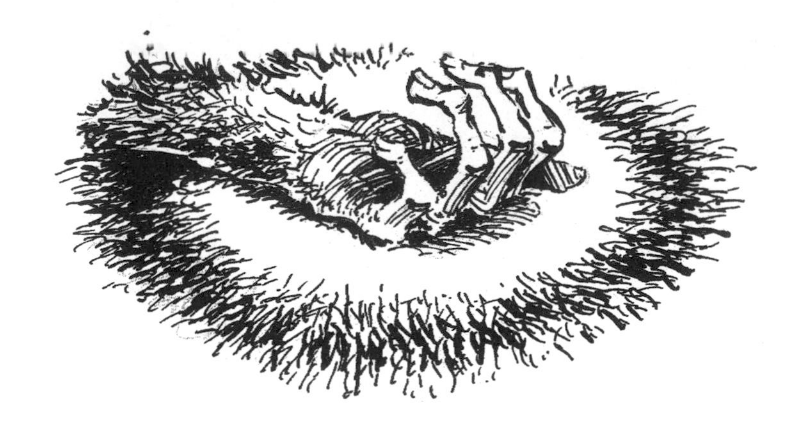

The Train Room

GARY HINES

The little man stood by the window in the third-floor tower room. One eye opened slowly. He watched as a limousine let out Wesley Hopkins. The little man did not move, which made sense. But the opening eye was truly odd. It had always been shut before. After all, it was painted on, typical for a train conductor made of wood.

"Is my room set up, Grandpop?" Wesley asked eagerly as he walked through the door of the mansion.

"Yes," his grandfather answered.

"Hooray!" Wesley shouted.

"Do you really think you should let him get so carried away with all this?" Wesley's father asked, coming in behind his son.

The older Mr. Hopkins stroked his chin and smiled slightly. "Oh, someday he'll learn our own actions come back to haunt us."

Wesley snatched his suitcase from his father's hand and, with a quick, "I'll see you tomorrow, Dad," dashed up the stairs to the third floor.

His room, the train room, was in one of the house's three towers. Wesley charged through the door. He clapped his hands and whooped.

The train tracks encircled the round room on a narrow table. The only opening was at the door where a drawbridge was raised to let him in.

He lowered the drawbridge, dropped his suitcase, and leaped knees first onto the bed, which sat precisely in the center of everything.

Good! he thought, noting his grandfather had replaced the two engines Wesley had wrecked during his last visit. Now there was a new red and silver Santa Fe diesel and a shiny, black steam locomotive with "Union Pacific" painted on the tender.

Wesley glanced out the window as his father's limousine drove off. "Out of the way, little man," he said, knocking the toy train conductor away from the tracks. He flicked on the electric transformer.

The Santa Fe pulled onto the main line as Wesley increased the power. Round the room it went, pulling four cars. Faster . . . faster.

Sparks flew from the caboose wheels—*Pop! Snap!*—as it bounced up and derailed, clunking to rest upside down across the track.

Wesley grinned and pushed the throttle. The locomotive whined as it tore around the room. Only its magnetic wheels kept it on the rails. Other cars came off, one at a time, until only the engine was left, screaming at full speed, bearing down on the helpless caboose. With a loud crash, the caboose careened to the floor as the sleek Santa Fe tipped over, slammed into the wall, and crunched to a stop.

"Wow! That was great!" Wesley shouted.

But across the room, facing Wesley's back, the little man slowly opened his eye once more.

Wesley slept peacefully, sprawled across his bed within the circle of track. His day had been full of wrecks.

It was late, past midnight.

And that's when it started, a faint, almost imperceptible scratching.

Scratch . . . scratch . . . (like a whisper) *scratch.*

Wesley rolled over.

Scratch . . . scratch.

Wesley lay still.

More scratching.

Wesley's eyes opened.

Had he heard something? Maybe not. He flopped on his belly.

Scratch . . . scratch . . . scratch.

There it is again.

Wesley rose up. He reached for the lamp and turned the switch. No light. Odd.

He stared into the darkness, then blinked his eyes. There, by the water tower, was a dim glow. Shaking his head, Wesley swallowed thickly and stood up, pulled toward the strange light.

It grew brighter, drawing him closer until a shape became clear. It was the little conductor, still as stone, bathed in the eerie glow. Wesley bent down.

Both the little man's eyes opened. Wesley jumped back.

The conductor raised his arm. "You!" he said.

Wesley's jaw dropped but no sound came out as the ghostly light enveloped him.

The little man grew and grew. So did the train tracks and the trains. Wesley's skin went clammy. His eyes rolled back and forth. Everything in the room was growing.

No. He was *shrinking*!

Panicked, Wesley tried to run, but like in a dream, nothing worked: not his arms, legs, hands, feet—nothing.

The little man watched, pleased, his arm still pointing at Wesley. And when Wesley had shrunken to the conductor's size, he found himself on the tracks, standing helplessly.

The conductor's eyes grew cold and his eyebrows rose scornfully. "You wreck us, Wesley Hopkins, now we wreck you!"

A loud click spat behind Wesley. He turned, gasping. The black steam engine, gigantic and powerful, hummed to life. Its headlamp caught Wesley in its light. Then the wheels began turning, spinning on the rails as they fought for traction.

Wesley stumbled to the side, trying to get off the tracks. He yelled as a chain-link fence hit him full in the face. Where had that come from? His railroad didn't have a fence. He spun around. All along the track, on both sides, was high fencing, too high to get over.

The locomotive moved, slowly, its wheels gripping and pistons groaning. Steam hissed from its belly. It was alive now, fully awake, and coming after him. Terrified, Wesley looked at it. Taking a step back and tripping, falling, pushing himself backward, he finally scrambled to his feet.

Wide eyed, mouth open, he turned and started running. His only escape was down the tracks.

Maybe I'll find an opening in the fence, he thought. *Maybe there'll be a place low enough to climb over.*

Maybe.

The shrill whistle blew. Wesley cried out, screams pouring from his mouth. Then somewhere, over the building noise, he heard laughter and looked up. Ahead, outside the fence, was the conductor, still pointing at Wesley and laughing.

The steam engine came closer, closer, and Wesley, running and gasping hard now, cried at every breath.

Squinting through his sweat, Wesley saw the conductor again, this time pointing down and away from him, down to the ground.

But it wasn't the ground he was pointing to, it was the edge of the table, the gigantic, high train table.

Wesley stumbled up and looked into the darkness. He spun around, wailing in fright as the giant steam beast surged toward him.

The conductor called out, "Jump! Jump!" and laughed again.

The locomotive swelled to a monstrous shadow that seemed to swallow up the sky. Wesley shrieked and toppled as the engine's cow catcher forced him over the edge and into the emptiness.

Wesley woke on the floor. Next to him was the little steam engine, turned on its side. Sunlight filled the room.

He gathered himself and sat up, shaking.

I must have fallen out of bed and somehow swiped the locomotive with my arm, he thought.

Across the room, next to the window, was the toy conductor. Wesley walked over cautiously. The little man was like he'd always been, both eyes closed and a smug look painted on his face. Wesley looked at him for a moment, then smiled and sighed deeply.

His father arrived a bit later to pick him up.

"How many do I have to replace this time?" Wesley's grandfather asked, hugging him goodbye.

Wesley smiled. "Just a couple. But that'll be it. I don't think I'll be wrecking trains anymore."

"Oh?" his grandfather asked, his brow lifting.

"I think playing *regular* trains might be more fun."

Wesley's grandfather opened the door of the third-floor train room and peered in. By the window, watching a limousine drive away, stood a little man. He smiled. This was odd. But odder still was the wink he exchanged with old Mr. Hopkins. After all, his mouth and eyes were only painted on, typical for a train conductor made of wood.

The Geebung Polo Club

BANJO PATERSON

It was somewhere up the country, in a land of rock and scrub,
That they formed an institution called the Geebung Polo Club.
They were long and wiry natives from the rugged mountain side,
And the horse was never saddled that the Geebungs couldn't ride;
But their style of playing polo was irregular and rash—
They had mighty little science, but a mighty lot of dash:
And they played on mountain ponies that were muscular and strong,
Though their coats were quite unpolished, and their manes and
tails were long.
And they used to train those ponies wheeling cattle in the scrub;
They were demons, were the members of the Geebung Polo Club.

It was somewhere down the country, in a city's smoke and steam,
That a polo club existed, called "The Cuff and Collar Team."
As a social institution 'twas a marvelous success,
For the members were distinguished by exclusiveness and dress.
They had natty little ponies that were nice, and smooth, and sleek,
For their cultivated owners only rode 'em once a week.
So they started up the country in pursuit of sport and fame,
For they meant to show the Geebungs how they ought to play
the game;
And they took their valets with them—just to give their boots a rub
Ere they started operations on the Geebung Polo Club.

Now my readers can imagine how the contest ebbed and flowed,
When the Geebung boys got going it was time to clear the road;
And the game was so terrific that ere half the time was gone
A spectator's leg was broken—just from merely looking on.
For they waddied one another till the plain was strewn with dead,
While the score was kept so even that they neither got ahead.
And the Cuff and Collar Captain, when he tumbled off to die
Was the last surviving player—so the the game was called a tie.

Then the Captain of the Geebungs raised him slowly from the ground,
Though his wounds were mostly mortal, yet he fiercely gazed around;
There was no one to oppose him—all the rest were in a trance,
So he scrambled on his pony for his last expiring chance,
For he meant to make an effort to get victory to his side;
So he struck at goal—and missed it—then he tumbled off and died.

By the old Campaspe River, where the breezes shake the grass,
There's a row of little gravestones that the stockmen never pass,
For they bear a rude inscription saying, "Stranger, drop a tear,
For the Cuff and Collar players and the Geebung boys lie here."
And on misty moonlit evenings, while the dingoes howl around,
You can see their shadows flitting down that phantom polo ground;
You can hear the loud collisions as the flying players meet,
And the rattle of the mallets, and the rush of ponies' feet,
Till the terrified spectator rides like blazes to the pub—
He's been haunted by the specters of the Geebung Polo Club.

The Doll's Ghost

MARION CRAWFORD

It was a terrible accident, and for one moment the splendid machinery of Cranston House got out of gear and stood still. The butler emerged from the retirement in which he spent his elegant leisure, two grooms of the chambers appeared simultaneously from opposite directions, there were actually housemaids on the grand staircase, and those who remember the facts most exactly assert that Mrs. Pringle herself positively stood upon the landing. Mrs. Pringle was the housekeeper. As for the head nurse, the under nurse, and the nursery-maid, their feelings cannot be described.

The Lady Gwendolen Lancaster-Douglas-Scroop, youngest daughter of the ninth Duke of Cranston, and aged six years and three months, picked herself up quite alone, and sat down on the third step of the grand staircase in Cranston House.

"Oh!" ejaculated the butler, and he disappeared again.

"Ah!" responded the grooms of the chambers, as they also went away.

"It's only that doll," Mrs. Pringle was distinctly heard to say, in a tone of contempt.

The under nurse heard her say it. Then the three nurses gathered round Lady Gwendolen and patted her, and gave her unhealthy things out of their pockets, and hurried her out of Cranston House as fast as they could, lest it should be found out upstairs that they had allowed the Lady Gwendolen Lancaster-Douglas-Scroop to tumble

down the grand staircase with her doll in her arms. And as the doll was badly broken, the nursery-maid carried it, with the pieces, wrapped up in Lady Gwendolen's little cloak. It was not far to Hyde Park, and when they had reached a quiet place they took means to find out that Lady Gwendolen had no bruises. For the carpet was very thick and soft, and there was thick stuff under it to make it softer.

Lady Gwendolen Douglas-Scroop sometimes yelled, but she never cried. It was because she had yelled that the nurse had allowed her to go downstairs alone with Nina, the doll, under one arm, while she steadied herself with her other hand on the balustrade, and trod upon the polished marble steps beyond the edge of the carpet. So she had fallen, and Nina had come to grief…

Mr. Bernard Puckler and his little daughter lived in a little house in a little alley, which led out off a quiet little street not very far from Belgrave Square. He was the great doll doctor, and his extensive practice lay in the most aristocratic quarter. He mended dolls of all sizes and ages, boy dolls and girl dolls, baby dolls in long clothes, and grown-up dolls in fashionable gowns, talking dolls and dumb dolls, those that shut their eyes when they lay down, and those whose eyes had to be shut for them by means of a mysterious wire. His daughter Else was only just over twelve years old, but she was already very clever at mending dolls' clothes, and at doing their hair, which is harder than you might think, though the dolls sit quite still while it is being done.

Mr. Puckler had originally been a German,

but he had dissolved his nationality in the ocean of London many years ago, like a great many foreigners. He still had one or two German friends, however, who came on Saturday evenings and smoked with him and played picquet or "skat" with him for farthing points, and called him "Herr Doctor," which seemed to please Mr. Puckler very much.

He looked older than he was, for his beard was rather long and ragged, his hair was grizzled and thin, and he wore horn-rimmed spectacles.

As for Else, she was a thin, pale child, very quiet and neat, with dark eyes and brown hair that was plaited down her back and tied with a bit of black ribbon. She mended the dolls' clothes and took the dolls back to their homes when they were quite strong again.

The house was a little one, but too big for the two people who lived in it. There was a small sitting-room on the street, and the workshop was at the back, and there were three rooms upstairs. But the father and daughter lived most of their time in the workshop, because they were generally at work, even in the evenings.

Mr. Puckler laid Nina on the table and looked at her a long time, till the tears began to fill his eyes behind the horn-rimmed spectacles. He was a very susceptible man, and he often fell in love with the dolls he mended, and found it hard to part with them when they had smiled at him for a few days. They were real little people to him, with characters and thoughts and feelings of their own, and he was very tender with them all. But some attracted him especially from the first, and when they were brought to him maimed and injured, their state seemed so pitiful to him that the tears came easily. You must remember that he had lived among dolls during a great part of his life, and understood them.

"How do you know that they feel nothing?" he went on to say to Else. "You must be gentle with them. It costs nothing to be kind to the little beings, and perhaps it makes a difference to them."

And Else understood him, because she was a child, and she knew that she was more to him than all the dolls.

He fell in love with Nina at first sight, perhaps because her beautiful brown glass eyes were something like Else's own, and he loved Else first and best, with all his heart. And, besides, it was a very sorrowful case. Nina had evidently not been long in the world, for her complexion was perfect, her hair was smooth where it should be smooth, and curly where it should be curly, and her silk clothes were perfectly new. But across her face was that frightful gash, like a sabre-cut, deep and shadowy within, but clean and sharp at the edges. When he tenderly pressed her head to close the gaping wound, the edges made a fine, grating sound, that was painful to hear, and the lids of the dark eyes quivered and trembled as though Nina were suffering dreadfully.

"Poor Nina!" he exclaimed sorrowfully. "But I shall not hurt you much, though you will take a long time to get strong."

He always asked the names of the broken dolls when they were brought to him, and sometimes the people knew what the children called them, and told him. He liked "Nina" for a name. Altogether and in every way she pleased him more than any doll he had seen for many years, and he felt drawn to her, and made up his mind to make her perfectly strong and sound, no matter how much labor it might cost him.

Mr. Puckler worked patiently a little at a time, and Else watched him. She could do nothing for poor Nina, whose clothes needed no mending. The longer the doll doctor worked, the more fond he became of the yellow hair and the beautiful brown glass eyes. He sometimes forgot all the other dolls that were waiting to be mended, lying side by side on a shelf, and sat for an hour gazing at Nina's face, while he racked his ingenuity for some new invention by which to hide even the smallest trace of the terrible accident.

She was wonderfully mended. Even he was obliged to admit

that; but the scar was still visible to his keen eyes, a very fine line right across the face, downward from right to left. Yet all the conditions had been most favorable for a cure, since the cement had set quite hard at the first attempt and the weather had been fine and dry, which makes a great difference in a dolls' hospital.

At last he knew that he could do no more, and the under nurse had already come twice to see whether the job was finished, as she coarsely expressed it.

"Nina is not quite strong yet," Mr. Puckler had answered each time, for he could not make up his mind to face the parting.

And now he sat before the square deal table at which he worked, and Nina lay before him for the last time with a big brown paper box beside her. It stood there like her coffin, waiting for her, he thought. He must put her into it, and lay tissue paper over her dear face, and then put on the lid, and at the thought of tying the string his sight was dim with tears again. He was never to look into the glassy depths of the beautiful brown eyes any more, nor to hear the little wooden voice say "Pa-pa" and "Ma-ma." It was a very painful moment.

In the vain hope of gaining time before the separation, he took up the little sticky bottles of cement and glue and gum and color, looking at each one in turn, and then at Nina's face. And all his small tools lay there, neatly arranged in a row, but he knew that he could not use them again for Nina. She was quite strong at last, and in a country where there should be no cruel children to hurt her she might live a hundred years, with only that almost imperceptible line across her face, to tell of the fearful thing that had befallen her on the marble steps of Cranston House.

Suddenly Mr. Puckler's heart was quite full, and he rose abruptly from his seat and turned away.

"Else," he said unsteadily, "you must do it for me. I cannot bear to see her go into the box."

So he went and stood at the window with his back turned, while Else did what he had not the heart to do.

"Is it done?" he asked, not turning round. "Then take her away, my dear. Put on your hat, and take her to Cranston House quickly, and when you are gone I will turn round."

Else was used to her father's queer ways with the dolls, and though she had never seen him so much moved by a parting, she was not much surprised.

"Come back quickly," he said, when he heard her hand on the latch. "It is growing late, and I should not send you at this hour. But I cannot bear to look forward to it any more."

When Else was gone, he left the window and sat down in his place before the table again, to wait for the child to come back. He touched the place where Nina had lain, very gently, and he recalled the softly-tinted pink face, and the glass eyes, and the ringlets of yellow hair, till he could almost see them.

The evenings were long, for it was late in the spring. But it began to grow dark soon, and Mr. Puckler wondered why Else did not come back. She had been gone an hour and a half, and that was much longer than he had expected, for it was barely half a mile from Belgrave Square to Cranston House. He reflected that the child might have been kept waiting, but as the twilight deepened he grew anxious, and walked up and down in the dim workshop, no longer thinking of Nina, but of Else, his own living child, whom he loved.

An indefinable, disquieting sensation came upon him by fine degrees, a chilliness and a faint stirring of his thin hair, joined with a wish to be in any company rather than to be alone much longer. It was the beginning of fear.

He told himself in strong German-English that he was a foolish old man, and he began to feel about for the matches in the dusk. He knew just where they should be, for he always kept them in the same place, close to the little tin box that held bits of sealing-wax of various colors, for some kinds of mending. But somehow he could not find the matches in the gloom.

Something had happened to Else, he was sure, and as his fear increased, he felt as though it might be allayed if he could get a light and see what time it was. Then he called himself a foolish old man again, and the sound of his own voice startled him in the dark. He could not find the matches.

The window was gray still; he might see what time it was if he went close to it, and he could go and get matches out of the cupboard afterward. He stood back from the table, to get out of the way of the chair, and began to cross the board floor.

Something was following him in the dark. There was a small pattering, as of tiny feet upon the boards. He stopped and listened, and the roots of his hair tingled. It was nothing and he was a foolish old man. He made two steps more, and he was sure that he heard the little pattering again. He turned his back to the window, leaning against the sash so that the panes began to crack, and he faced the dark. Everything was quite still, and it smelt of paste and cement and wood-filings as usual.

"Is that you, Else?" he asked, and he was surprised by the fear in his voice.

There was no answer in the room, and he held up his watch and tried to make out what time it was by the gray dusk that was just not darkness. So far as he could see, it was within two or three minutes of ten o'clock. He had been a long time alone. He was shocked, and frightened for Else, out in London, so late, and he almost ran across the room to the door. As he fumbled for the latch, he distinctly heard the running of the little feet after him.

"Mice!" he exclaimed feebly, just as he got the door open.

He shut it quickly behind him, and felt as though some cold thing had settled on his back and were writhing upon him. The passage was quite dark, but he found his hat and was out in the alley in a moment, breathing more freely, and surprised to find how much light there still was in the open air. He could see the pavement clearly under his feet, and far off in the street to which the alley led he could hear the laughter and calls of children, playing some game out of doors. He wondered how he could have been so nervous, and for an instant he thought of going back into the house to wait quietly for Else. But instantly he felt that nervous fright of something stealing over him again. In any case it was better to walk up to Cranston House and ask the servants about the child. One of the women had perhaps taken a fancy to her, and was even now giving her tea and cake.

He walked quickly to Belgrave Square, and then up the broad streets, listening as he went, whenever there was no other sound, for the tiny footsteps. But he heard nothing, and was laughing at himself when he rang the servants' bell at the big house. Of course, the child must be there.

The person who opened the door was quite an inferior person—for it was a back door—but affected the manners of the front, and stared at Mr. Puckler superciliously.

No little girl had been seen, and he knew "nothing about no dolls."

"She is my little girl," said Mr. Puckler tremulously, for all his anxiety was returning tenfold, "and I am afraid something has happened."

The inferior person said rudely that "nothing could have happened to her in that house, because she had not been there, which was a jolly good reason why"; and Mr. Puckler was obliged to admit that the man ought to know, as it was his business to keep the door and let people in. He wished to be allowed to speak to the under nurse, who knew him; but the man was ruder than ever, and finally shut the door in his face.

When the doll doctor was alone in the street, he steadied

himself by the railing, for he felt as though he were breaking in two, just as some dolls break, in the middle of the backbone.

Presently he knew that he must be doing something to find Else, and that gave him strength. He began to walk as quickly as he could through the streets, following every highway and byway which his little girl might have taken on her errand. He also asked several policemen in vain if they had seen her, and most of them answered him kindly, for they saw that he was a sober man and in his right senses, and some of them had little girls of their own.

It was one o'clock in the morning when he went up to his own door again, worn out and hopeless and broken-hearted. As he turned

the key in the lock, his heart stood still, for he knew that he was awake and not dreaming, and that he really heard those tiny footsteps pattering to meet him inside the house along the passage.

But he was too unhappy to be much frightened any more, and his heart went on again with a dull regular pain, that found its way all through him with every pulse. So he went in and hung up his hat in the dark, and found the matches in the cupboard and the candlestick in its place in the corner.

Mr. Puckler was so much overcome and so completely worn out that he sat down in his chair before the worktable and almost fainted, as his face dropped forward upon his folded hands. Beside him the solitary candle burned steadily with a low flame in the still warm air.

"Else! Else!" he moaned against his yellow knuckles. And that was all he could say, and it was no relief to him. On the contrary, the very sound of the name was a new and sharp pain that pierced his ears and his head and his very soul. For every time he repeated the name it meant that little Else was dead, somewhere out in the streets of London in the dark.

He was so terribly hurt that he did not even feel something pulling gently at the skirt of his old coat, so gently that it was like the nibbling of a tiny mouse. He might have thought that it was really a mouse if he had noticed it.

"Else! Else!" he groaned, right against his hands.

Then a cool breath stirred his thin hair, and the low flame of the one candle dropped down almost to a mere spark, not flickering as though a draught were going to blow it out, but just dropping down as if it were tired out. Mr. Puckler felt his hands stiffening with fright under his face; and there was a faint rustling sound, like some small silk thing blown in a gentle breeze. He sat up straight, stark and scared, and a small wooden voice spoke in the stillness.

"Pa-pa," it said, with a break between the syllables.

Mr. Puckler stood up in a single jump, and his chair fell over backward with a smashing noise upon the wooden floor. The candle had almost gone out.

It was Nina's doll-voice that had spoken, and he should have known it among the voices of a hundred other dolls. And yet there was something more in it, a little human ring, with a pitiful cry and a call for help, and the wail of a hurt child. Mr. Puckler stood up, stark and stiff, and tried to look round, but at first he could not, for he seemed to be frozen from head to foot.

Then he made a great effort, and he raised one hand to each of his temples, and pressed his own head round as he would have turned a doll's. The candle was burning so low that it might as well have been out altogether, for any light it gave, and the room seemed quite dark at first. Then he saw something. He would not have believed that he could be more frightened than he had been just before that. But he was, and his knees shook, for he saw the doll standing in the middle of the floor, shining with a faint and ghostly radiance, her beautiful glassy brown eyes fixed on his. And across her face the very thin line of the break he had mended shone as though it were drawn in light with a fine point of white flame.

Yet there was something more in the eyes, too; there was something human, like Else's own, but as if only the doll saw him through them, and not Else. And there was enough of Else to bring back all his pain and to make him forget his fear.

"Else! My little Else!" he cried aloud.

The small ghost moved, and its doll-arm slowly rose and fell with a stiff, mechanical motion.

"Pa-pa," it said.

It seemed this time that there was even more of Else's tone echoing somewhere between the wooden notes that reached his ears so distinctly and yet so far away. Else was calling him, he was sure.

His face was perfectly white in the gloom, but his knees did not shake any more, and he felt that he was less frightened.

"Yes, child! But where? Where?" he asked. "Where are you, Else!"

"Pa-pa!"

The syllables died away in the quiet room.

There was a low rustling of silk, the glassy brown eyes turned slowly away, and Mr. Puckler heard the pitter-patter of the small feet in the bronze kid slippers as the figure ran straight to the door. Then the candle burned high again, the room was full of light, and he was alone.

Mr. Puckler passed his hand over his eyes and looked about him. He could see everything quite clearly, and he felt that he must have been dreaming, though he was standing instead of sitting down, as he should have been if he had just waked up. The candle burned brightly now. There were the dolls to be mended, lying in a row with their toes up. The third one had lost her right shoe, and Else was making one. He knew that, and he was certainly not dreaming now. He had not been dreaming when he had come in from his fruitless search and had heard the doll's footsteps running to the door. He had not fallen asleep in his chair. How could he possibly have fallen asleep, when his heart was breaking? He had been awake all the time.

He steadied himself, set the fallen chair upon its legs, and said to himself again very emphatically that he was a foolish old man. He ought to be out in the streets looking for his child, asking

questions, and inquiring at the police stations, where all accidents were reported as soon as they were known, or at the hospitals.

"Pa-pa!"

The longing, wailing, pitiful little wooden cry rang from the passage, outside the door, and Mr. Puckler stood for an instant with white face, transfixed and rooted to the spot. A moment later his hand was on the latch. Then he was in the passage, with the

light streaming from the open door behind him.

Quite at the other end he saw the little phantom shining clearly in the shadow, and the right hand seemed to beckon to him as the arm rose and fell once more. He knew all at once that it had not come to frighten him but to lead him, and when it disappeared, and he walked boldly towards the door, he knew that it was in the street outside, waiting for him. He forgot that he was tired and had eaten no supper, and had walked many miles, for a sudden hope ran through and through him, like a golden stream of life.

And sure enough, at the corner of the alley, and at the corner of the street, and out in Belgrave Square, he saw the small ghost flitting before him. Sometimes it was only a shadow, where there was other light, but then the glare of the lamps made a pale green sheen on its little Mother Hubbard frock of silk; and sometimes, where the streets were dark and silent, the whole figure shone out brightly, with its yellow curls and rosy neck. It seemed to trot along like a tiny child, and Mr. Puckler could hear the pattering of the bronze kid slippers on the pavement as it ran. But it went very fast, and he could only just keep up with it, tearing along with his hat on the back of his head and his thin hair blown by the night breeze, and his horn-rimmed spectacles firmly set upon his broad nose.

On and on he went, and he had no idea where he was. He did not even care, for he knew certainly that he was going the right way.

Then at last, in a wide, quiet street, he was standing before a big, sober-looking door that had two lamps on each side of it, and a polished brass bell-handle, which he pulled.

And just inside, where the door was opened, in the bright light, there was the little shadow, and the pale green sheen of the little silk dress, and once more the small cry came to his ears, less pitiful, more longing.

"Pa-pa!"

The shadow turned suddenly bright, and out of the brightness the beautiful brown glass eyes were turned up happily to his, while the rosy mouth smiled so divinely that the phantom doll looked almost like a little angel just then.

"A little girl was brought in soon after ten o'clock," said the quiet voice of the hospital doorkeeper. "I think they thought she was only stunned. She was holding a big brown-paper box against her, and they could not get it out of her arms. She had a long plait of brown hair that hung down as they carried her."

"She is my little girl," said Mr. Puckler, but he hardly heard his own voice.

He leaned over Else's face in the gentle light of the children's ward, and when he had stood there a minute the beautiful brown eyes opened and looked up to his.

"Pa-pa!" cried Else softly, "I knew you would come!"

Then Mr. Puckler did not know what he did or said for a moment, and what he felt was worth all the fear and terror and despair that had almost killed him that night. But by and by Else was telling her story, and the nurse let her speak, for there were only two other children in the room, who were getting well and were sound asleep.

"They were big boys with bad faces," said Else, "and they tried to get Nina away from me, but I held on and fought as well as I could till one of them hit me with something, and I don't remember any more, for I tumbled down and I suppose the boys ran away, and somebody found me there. But I'm afraid Nina is all smashed."

"Here is the box," said the nurse. "We could not take it out of her arms till she came to herself. Would you like to see if the doll is broken?"

And she undid the string cleverly, but Nina was all smashed to pieces. Only the gentle light of the children's ward made a pale green sheen in the folds of the little Mother Hubbard frock.

Lizard: The Devil's Plaything

KAREN VOSS PETERS

Man, did I feel sorry for Tommy Marshall. He's the new kid in class. Ever since he started at our school, the other kids have made his life miserable. My desk is two seats behind and one row over from Tommy's so I usually see everything that happens to him. When he tried to give a speech on lizards his words were drowned out by kids coughing and sneezing loudly. No one could hear anything he said. He stood there so angry, his face all red and his fists clenched. But that didn't stop the other kids from making fun of him. He finally gave up, stopping in mid-sentence when one of Boyd's spit balls hit him in the face landing right on the forehead. Boyd's aim was the best in the class. Tommy marched over to him and was about to smack him in the nose when the bell rang.

I caught up to Tommy after class just as he was slamming his locker shut and asked if I could walk home with him. When he shrugged, I took this to mean yes. He still didn't say too much; we must have walked four blocks before he finally said something.

"Your speech on car racing was pretty good."

"Not as good as yours on lizards," I said.

"Yeah, like you could hear it."

"I heard most of it," I said trying my best to cheer him up. "Do you really have a lizard?"

He nodded. "A type of lizard," he said vaguely. "My dad brought her back from South America. He's a famous scientist and does research all over the world. He usually brings back some kind of pet for me. You can see my lizard if you want to."

Do you ever have the feeling someone is lying—or at least, exaggerating? That's how I felt now, but I didn't challenge Tommy because I really did want to see the lizard or whatever it was.

I felt more sorry for Tommy Marshall when I saw the house he lived in—more like a glorified shed. Couldn't have had more than two bedrooms at the most, and small at that. If his dad was so great, why could they only afford a shack to live in? I didn't want to give Tommy a hard time so I didn't ask any questions. I didn't get a chance to look in any of the other rooms as he led me down a short hall into his bedroom.

It was as cluttered as mine was but not with the stuff typical of a twelve-year-old. Sure, he had jars and aquariums like most boys but these were filled with dried-up lizard looking creatures.

"Are these all dead?" I asked, picking up a jar to see if there was anything under the leaves and twigs.

He took it from me. "I was trying to breed different species together but it hasn't worked. They just keep dying. Do you want to see Chow-down or not?"

"Chow-down?"

"Here she is." He reached for something, on a shelf. It was dark red, the color of blood that comes from a deep gash. Its eyes were brilliant green and it was about six inches long with spiked things that ran along its spine from just behind its head to the tip of its tail.

Wow was all I could say. This was not the kind of lizard I was used to seeing. He held it out to me.

"Will it bite me?" I asked nervously. Tommy's lip curled and I knew he was thinking I was making a fuss like a baby. I wanted to tell him I handled lizards all the time just not one that looked like this.

"Take her but slowly. No sudden movements otherwise you'll spook her."

Great, I thought, that's all I need to hear. I reached out very slowly. The lizard turned her head towards my hand, blinking.

"I hope she knows I'm friendly," I said trying to laugh. Tommy rubbed his forefinger up and down each of the spikes on Chow-down's spine.

"Does that calm her?" I asked as my hand got closer to Chow-down's head. Tommy just shrugged. Thinking of something else to say, I said, "How did your dad get her through customs? I didn't think you were allowed to bring animals or insects into the country."

"It was easy. Chow-down was just a baby then, so my dad just stuck her in his pocket. No problem."

It seemed strange that a scientist would do something devious like that—why wouldn't he just get permission by saying it was for a research project?—but then I didn't know the hassles of crossing borders. I put my finger on the top of Chow-down's head trying to keep my touch gentle. But not gentle enough it seemed, for she suddenly turned her head and spat. It frightened me because I wasn't expecting it. I jumped back. On the back of my hand was a blob of green, sticky ooze.

"What is it?" I asked worried that my skin might shrivel up.

"You're such a baby," said Tommy, snatching the lizard out of my reach and putting her back on the shelf. "Why don't you just go running home to mother."

"I was startled that's all," I said. "Anyway, I have to get home now." I didn't wait to hear his answer because I was anxious to get out of there, for I had decided there was something definitely scary about Tommy Marshall and his weird pet.

He didn't have much to say to me the next morning at school but it didn't bother me. I had tried to be a friend and if he wasn't going to be decent back that was his business. Mrs. Stackpole, our teacher, planned to have more kids say their speeches, which gave me a chance to do my science homework for next class.

Boyd Fraser was the next victim to speak, but I was too involved in science calculations to listen until the class started laughing. I looked up and saw Boyd covering the front of his pants with his hands, trying to hide the wet stain that was slowly spreading down his pant legs. A pool gathered slowly at his feet. The kids laughed loudly at Boyd's embarrassment. He had bullied most of us at one time or another so no one felt sorry for him now. He was getting what he deserved. Tommy was the only one not joining in the fun. He was just sitting quietly moving his finger up and down in Boyd's direction. I watched as he moved his finger higher so it was in line with Boyd's face. Green slime trickled from Boyd's nose down onto his lips. The kids went crazy at this new development. They were pounding on their desks and clapping their hands. Mrs. Stackpole had to take the yard stick and slam it against the blackboard to restore order to the class. Tommy looked around at me and sneered. Poor Boyd ran from the room and didn't return to school for three days.

It was several days later before Tommy spoke to me again. Maybe he'd had a change of heart because he asked me if I wanted to go

to his house again. I hesitated, not sure if I wanted to get involved with this boy, but everyone deserves a second chance so I agreed. It would also give me a chance to show him I was not the coward he thought I was.

The house was empty again, prompting me to ask if I would get to meet his dad.

"Naw, he's away working on a project. It's just you and me."

I don't know why I shivered when he said that but I did.

"I have to feed Chow-down. She doesn't like to wait too long for her food. Do you want to do it?"

"Sure, what does she eat? Lettuce or something." I reached for a jar of lettuce that was on the desk.

"She hates that junk," Tommy said grabbing my hand. His fingers felt cold and rough. "Here's what my baby likes."

He handed me a shallow plastic dish and I peeled back the lid. I almost threw up at the sight of maggots, grubs and millipedes writhing in the dish. The smell was awful.

"Do you have a spoon or something?" I asked.

Tommy laughed. "You don't need a spoon, just pick 'em up with your fingers, one by one, though we don't want Chow-down to choke. Set them right in the middle of her tongue and she'll do the rest. Won't you, baby?" He was already cradling Chow-down in the palm of his hand. Tommy must have sensed my nervousness. "Watch me and then do the same thing."

He picked up a maggot with his forefinger and thumb and held it to Chow-down's nose. The lizard opened her jaws wide. As soon as she felt the morsel on her tongue, she snapped her jaws shut.

"You got to be quick otherwise you'll lose your finger," Tommy warned.

"I can see that," I said, wishing I hadn't agreed to this.

I picked up a grub, trying not to think about its slimy body squirming between my fingers. Imitating Tommy, I held the food out to Chow-down waiting for her to sniff it. I could feel her rough skin. She opened her mouth wide, and with a trembling hand I set the grub on Chow-down's pink tongue. I don't remember what happened next except for the pain. I do remember Tommy yelling at me, saying it was my fault for dropping the grub instead of placing it carefully in Chow-down's mouth. It doesn't matter anyway, what matters is that Chow-down locked her jaws together with my finger and thumb still in her mouth. I screamed. Tommy grabbed another grub from the bowl and offered it to Chow-down. The trick worked except my hand was minus a fingertip and my thumb hung in a bloody, shredded mess. That's when I fainted.

When I regained consciousness, I was lying on Tommy's bed. He was poking through an assortment of creams and bandages in a box.

"Don't you think I should go to the hospital?" I said.

He dismissed my suggestion. "I'll fix you up."

"But it hurts like hell," I whined.

He gave me a withering look. "You are such a baby." He walked over to Chow-down and ran his fingers up and down each of the spikes right along her back to the tip of her tail. Then he took my hand and touched the end of my finger and mangled thumb. It felt like someone putting cold ice on me.

"The pain's gone," I said in surprise. "How'd you do that?"

He shrugged as usual to my question. "I'll stick all the bits of your thumb back together with this bandage and it'll be fine in a few days. If anyone asks just say you were playing with an electric knife or something. Okay?" I was too nervous to argue, nodding in agreement. He gave me such a creepy feeling I just wanted to get away from him and his vicious lizard. When he put his hand on my arm I thought he wasn't going to let me leave.

"I'll walk with you just to make sure you get home safely. You look a little pale."

You'd look white too if half your finger and thumb was in Chow-down's belly, I thought. I tried to talk him out of walking with me but he insisted.

"Just keep that thing away from me," I said, pointing to

Chow-down as he plucked the lizard from the shelf and set her on his shoulder.

"You're not blaming Chow-down for what happened, are you? It wasn't her fault you were too slow."

There was obviously no arguing with him, so I didn't try. The sooner I was home the better.

The street was busy with people anxious to get home. Like my dad who always rushes home after work, hungry for his supper and television programs.

"Watch this," Tommy said.

At first I wasn't sure what he wanted me to see. There was a group of people getting on a bus. An old man was reaching forward to grab the bus rail to pull himself onto the first step. The bus lurched away from the curb. I watched in horror as the man was dragged down the road.

"Let go," I yelled even though I knew he couldn't possibly hear me.

People were running alongside of the bus, pounding on its side to catch the driver's attention. Tommy just laughed. He raised his hand and waved it in circles in the air. Two of the bus's tires blew, causing the bus to skid into the intersection where it was hit by a van. Everyone started running toward the accident.

I slapped Tommy's shoulder. "You did that, you creep."

His expression was innocent. "Why do you say that?" he said.

"Because I just know you did. You, and that thing," I said pointing at Chow-down. She was no ordinary lizard.

Tommy's eyes narrowed to slits. "I wouldn't go saying bad things about Chow-down. She doesn't like to be insulted and neither do I."

I ran. Just took off as fast I could. My house was just at the bottom of the hill and around the corner. It was the end house of a street that ran parallel to the train yard. If I could just get home, I'd be safe. Plans swirled through my head as I ran. As soon as I got home I would ask my mother to take me to the hospital. Then I would call the police and tell them about the bus and ask if the old man was all right. Then I would tell the school about Tommy. I just hoped people would believe me. My problem now was escaping him for I could sense him catching up to me.

I saw my house, yet when I got closer I couldn't stop. I just kept running, right past the front door. I glanced at it out of the corner of my eye but I couldn't stop. I ran to the end of the street, toward the train tracks. There were always boxcars parked on the tracks waiting to be loaded. I'd lived in this area so long, the train schedule was etched into my brain. I scooted around a line of box-cars and crouched down. I had to get my breath back for the ache in my side was unbearable. It was hard to hear anything over my gasps for breath not that it mattered for Tommy was suddenly standing beside me. He wasn't even breathing hard. Chow-down was still perched on his shoulder.

"You don't learn, do you? You can't escape me. We're friends and friends always stick together." He spoke softly and slowly.

"I'm not your friend," I shouted leaping up and shoving him backward. A thrill of pleasure shot through me as he staggered backward causing Chow-down to slip from his shoulder. She clung to his sleeve. I didn't wait to see the rest but ran alongside of the freight cars until I found one with the doors open. I climbed in and leaned on the door bar with all my strength to close it. My relief was short-lived as, with inches to spare, I saw Tommy's hand reach around the end of the door and the gap widen. It became a battle of strength with both of us pushing on the door in different directions. Chow-down jumped down from Tommy's arm and scurried toward me. I glanced at the lizard squatting before me, an uneasy feeling coming over me, and in that split second a stream of clear liquid squirted into my eyes. I dropped to my knees and covered my burning eyes with my hands, hearing the door scrape open and Tommy climbing in.

"If you're going to be my friend, you're going to have to toughen up," he whispered in my ear. I could feel his stinky breath on my neck. "Don't worry about your eyes. You'll be able to see in a few minutes."

He was right about my being able to see for my vision cleared after I blinked a few times. But he was dead wrong if he thought we were going to be friends.

When I could see again, he was sitting cross-legged on the floor feeding Chow-down worms which he took from his pocket. As he dangled the worms in front of the lizard's mouth, she would bite off a piece, swallow it and then open her mouth for more. It was then I got my idea—how to get Tommy out of my life once and for all.

"Can I feed her?"

Tommy looked suspicious at my offer. "I didn't think you wanted to have anything to do with her."

"Oh she's not so bad," I said, "maybe I did spook her before. Put her down on the ground and I'll feed her. It might be better if I don't hold her."

He didn't argue and set Chow-down on the floor. The lizard seemed upset that her meal had been interrupted and made a squawking noise in protest. I rolled onto my stomach opposite her and took the grub which Tommy handed to me. This time I didn't flinch at touching the slimy bug. Chow-down seemed relaxed too. Holding my breath, I put the grub into Chow-down's mouth and quickly drew back my hand. No problems. I fed her three grubs like this before taking a quick look at Tommy, then I ran my finger along Chow-down's spine, up and down each spike.

"Hey, what're you doing?" Tommy grasped my wrist.

"What's your problem?" I said flinging off his hand. "I'm just stroking her while she eats. I want her to know I won't hurt her."

"I'm the only one that strokes her," he said.

"Why, because it gives you special powers?" As I said this, I jumped up and pointed my finger at him willing him to fall backward. To my astonishment, he did. That was the secret. I seized Chow-down and headed for the open door. Before I had a chance to jump, I was hurled to one side. The train had started to move forward with a lurching motion. Tommy fell toward me.

"Give her back to me," he shouted.

"Never," I yelled.

With the movement of the train it was hard to keep my balance, so I crawled towards the door with Chow-down still in my grasp. Tommy straddled my back, clamping his legs into my sides so hard it was difficult to breathe. We rocked back and forth a few times as I tried to make him fall off, but his grip was tight. I tried pointing my finger over my shoulder in his direction but nothing happened. Maybe the powers only worked for a short time.

The train was moving smoother as it increased its speed. The scenery was whipping past us as we headed out of town. Tommy was swearing as he struggled to get back his lizard. He slapped my head so hard, tears blurred my vision. He tried pulling back my fingers, which were fastened around Chow-down's body, but I still didn't let go. I was starting to weaken.

Letting my body go limp I said I would give him Chow-down if he would get off my back.

"That's better," he said. As soon as I was free of him, I stood up and waved Chow-down in the air.

"Come and get her," I said. Bending over, he roared loudly and butted me in the stomach with his head, knocking us both out of the box-car and slamming us onto the ground. I landed hard on gravel. Still hanging onto each other, we rolled over and over down an embankment, finally stopping when we crashed against some boulders.

My bones were aching and I had cuts and scrapes on my arms and face that were bleeding. I was amazed to see I was still holding Chow-down, who didn't appear to be injured in any way. Tommy was lying still. I inched my way over to him not sure if he was faking it and would suddenly leap at me. He was lying on his back.

Kneeling beside him, I looked carefully over his body. He didn't even have scrapes and bruises. Wondering if he had banged his head, I turned him to one side and touched the back of his head. I almost fainted at what I saw. There was a large opening from the base of his neck about the size of an orange. I took big gulps of air to steady my trembling body and then put my finger in the hole. Nothing. I couldn't feel anything, no blood, no bones, no veins, nothing. This was weird. I pulled back the skin and it peeled away off in my hand just like paper. I pulled back more. This was not an ordinary body. There was nothing inside the skin. My legs were shaking so much I had to sit back for a moment to catch my breath. I heard a rustling in the grass. Chow-down appeared. She was making the same squawking noise as before as she scurried onto Tommy's body. I felt sorry for her.

"It's okay, buddy," I said. I had to find out what Tommy really was because he certainly wasn't a boy.

I continued to rip the skin apart across his back, the hole became wider and wider. I almost jumped out of my own skin as I felt something under my hand. I waited. From out of the deep cavity I could see two eyes looking back at me. Then it came out.

A lizard, the same color and everything like Chow-down only about twice her size. I was too scared to move. Chow-down seemed pleased to see this new lizard for she climbed onto its back and nuzzled its head. I thought maybe it was Chow-down's mother. Obviously I couldn't leave the lizards here, nor did I want to really. The large lizard let me pick her up and tuck her under my arm. Chow-down, trusting me like an old friend in spite of everything, perched on my shoulder. I stroked her head.

"I'm going to look after you now," I said to her. I needed to get home and fix up my wounds, I thought as I touched a large cut on my arm. And in that instant, I watched the blood disappear and the cut close itself. It was then I realized—I was like Tommy Marshall now.

The Ride-by-Nights

WALTER DE LA MARE

Up on their brooms the Witches stream,
Crooked and black in the crescent's gleam;
One foot high, and one foot low,
Bearded, cloaked, and cowled, they go,
'Neath Charlie's Wain they twitter and tweet,
And away they swarm 'neath the Dragon's feet,
With a whoop and a flutter they swing and sway,
And surge pell-mell down the Milky Way.
Betwixt the legs of the glittering Chair
They hover and squeak in the empty air.
Then round they swoop past the
glimmering Lion
To where Sirius barks
behind huge Orion:
Up, then, and over to
wheel amain,
Under the silver, and
home again.

The Kit-Bag

ALGERNON BLACKWOOD

When the words "Not guilty" sounded through the crowded courtroom that dark December afternoon, Arthur Wilbraham, the great criminal K.C., and leader for the triumphant defense, was represented by his junior: but Johnson, his private secretary, carried the verdict across to his chambers like lightning.

"It's what we expected, I think," said the barrister, without emotion; "and, personally, I am glad the case is over." There was no particular sign of pleasure that his defense of John Turk, the murderer, on a plea of insanity, had been successful, for no doubt he felt, as everybody who had watched the case felt, that no man had ever better deserved the gallows.

"I'm glad too," said Johnson. He had sat in the court for ten days watching the face of the man who had carried out with callous detail one of the most brutal and cold-blooded murders of recent years.

The counsel glanced up at his secretary. They were more than employer and employed; for family and other reasons, they were friends. "Ah, I remember; yes," he said with a kind smile, "and you want to get away for Christmas? You're going to skate and ski in the Alps, aren't you? If I was your age I'd come with you."

Johnson laughed shortly. He was a young man of twenty-six,

with a delicate face like a girl's. "I can catch the morning boat now," he said; "but that's not the reason I'm glad the trial is over. I'm glad it's over because I've seen the last of that man's dreadful face. It positively haunted me. That white skin, with the black hair brushed low over the forehead, is a thing I shall never forget, and the description of the way the dismembered body was crammed and packed with lime into that—"

"Don't dwell on it, my dear fellow," interrupted the other, looking at him curiously out of his keen eyes, "don't think about it. Such pictures have a trick of coming back when one least wants them." He paused a moment. "Now go," he added presently, "and enjoy your holiday. I shall want all your energy for my Parliamentary work when you get back. And don't break your neck skiing."

Johnson shook hands and took his leave. At the door he turned suddenly.

"I knew there was something I wanted to ask you," he said. "Would you mind lending me one of your kit-bags? It's too late to get one tonight, and I leave in the morning before the shops are open."

"Of course. I'll send Henry over with it to your rooms. You shall have it the moment I get home."

"I promise to take great care of it," said Johnson gratefully, delighted to think that within thirty hours he would be nearing the brilliant sunshine of the high Alps in winter. The thought of that criminal court was like an evil dream in his mind.

He dined at his club and went on to Bloomsbury, where he occupied the top floor in one of those old, gaunt houses in which the rooms are large and lofty. The floor below his own was vacant and unfurnished, and below that were other lodgers whom he did not know. It was cheerless, and he looked forward heartily to a change. The night was even more cheerless: it was miserable, and few people were about. A cold, sleety rain was driving down the streets before the keenest east wind he had ever felt. It howled dismally among the big, gloomy houses of the great squares, and when he reached his rooms he heard it whistling and shouting over the world of black roofs beyond his windows.

In the hall he met his landlady, shading a candle from the drafts with her thin hand. "This come by a man from Mr. Wilbr'im's, sir."

She pointed to what was evidently the kit-bag, and Johnson thanked her and took it upstairs with him. "I shall be going abroad in the morning for ten days, Mrs. Monks," he said. "I'll leave an address for letters."

"And I hope you'll 'ave a merry Christmas, sir," she said, in a raucous, wheezy voice that suggested spirits, "and better weather than this."

"I hope so too," replied her lodger, shuddering a little as the wind went roaring down the street outside.

When he got upstairs he heard the sleet volleying against the windowpanes. He put his kettle on to make a cup of hot coffee, and then set about putting a few things in order for his absence. "And now I must pack—such as my packing is," he laughed to himself, and set to work at once.

He liked the packing, for it brought the snow mountains so vividly before him, and made him forget the unpleasant scenes of the past ten days. Besides, it was not elaborate in nature. His friend had lent him the very thing—a stout canvas kit-bag, sack shaped, with holes around the neck for the brass bar and padlock. It was a bit shapeless, true, and not much to look at, but its capacity was unlimited, and there was no need to pack carefully. He shoved in his waterproof coat, his fur cap and gloves, his skates and climbing boots, his sweaters, snowboots, and ear-caps;

and then on the top of these he piled his woolen shirts and underwear, his thick socks, puttees, and knickerbockers. The dress suit came next, in case the hotel people dressed for dinner, and then, thinking of the best way to pack his white shirts, he paused a moment to reflect. "That's the worst of these kit-bags," he mused vaguely, standing in the center of the sitting room, where he had come to fetch some string.

It was after ten o'clock. A furious gust of wind rattled the windows as though to hurry him up, and he thought with pity of the poor Londoners whose Christmas would be spent in such a climate, whilst he was skimming over snowy slopes in bright sunshine, and dancing in the evening with rosy-cheeked girls—Ah! that reminded him; he must put in his dancing-pumps and evening socks. He crossed over from his sitting room to the cupboard on the landing where he kept his linen.

And as he did so he heard someone coming softly up the stairs.

He stood still a moment on the landing to listen. It was Mrs. Monks's step, he thought; she must be coming up with the last post. But then the steps ceased suddenly, and he heard no more. They were at least two flights down, and he came to the conclusion they were too heavy to be those of his bibulous landlady. No doubt they belonged to a late lodger who had mistaken his floor. He went into his bedroom and packed his pumps and dress shirts as best he could.

The kit-bag by this time was two-thirds full, and stood upright on its own base like a sack of flour. For the first time he noticed that it was old and dirty, the canvas faded and worn, and that it had obviously been subjected to rather rough treatment. It was not a very nice bag to have sent him—certainly not a new one, or one that his chief valued. He gave the matter a passing thought, and went on with his packing. Once or twice, however, he caught himself

wondering who it could have been wandering down below, for Mrs. Monks had not come up with letters, and the floor was empty and unfurnished. From time to time, moreover, he was almost certain he heard a soft tread of someone padding about over the bare boards—cautiously, stealthily, as silently as possible—and, further, that the sounds had been lately coming distinctly nearer.

For the first time in his life he began to feel a little creepy. Then, as though to emphasize this feeling, an odd thing happened: as he left the bedroom, having just packed his recalcitrant white shirts, he noticed that the top of the kit-bag lopped over toward him with an extraordinary resemblance to a human face. The canvas fell into a fold like a nose and forehead, and the brass rings for the padlock just filled the position of the eyes. A shadow—or was it a travel stain? for he could not tell exactly—looked like hair. It gave him rather a turn, for it was so absurdly, so outrageously, like the face of John Turk, the murderer.

He laughed, and went into the front room, where the light was stronger.

"That horrid case has got on my mind," he thought. "I shall be glad of a change of scene and air." In the sitting room, however, he was not pleased to hear again that stealthy tread upon the stairs, and to realize that it was much closer than before, as well as unmistakably real. And this time he got up and went out to see who it could be creeping about on the upper staircase at so late an hour.

But the sound ceased; there was no one visible on the stairs. He went to the floor below, not without trepidation, and turned on the electric light to make sure that no one was hiding in the empty rooms of the unoccupied suite. There was not a stick of furniture large enough to hide a dog. Then he called over the banisters to Mrs. Monks, but there was no answer, and his voice echoed down into the dark vault of the house, and was lost in the roar of the gale that howled outside. Everyone was in bed and asleep—everyone except himself and the owner of this soft and stealthy tread.

"My absurd imagination, I suppose," he thought. "It must have been the wind after all, although—it seemed so *very* real and close, I thought." He went back to his packing. It was by this time getting on toward midnight. He drank his coffee up and lit another pipe—the last before turning in.

It is difficult to say exactly at what point fear begins, when the causes of that fear are not plainly before the eyes. Impressions gather on the surface of the mind, film by film, as ice gathers upon the surface of still water, but often so lightly that they claim no definite recognition from the consciousness. Then a point is reached where the accumulated impressions become a definite emotion, and the mind realizes that something has happened. With something of a start, Johnson suddenly recognized that he felt nervous—oddly nervous; also, that for some time past, the causes of this feeling had been gathering slowly in his mind, but that he had only just reached the point where he was forced to acknowledge them.

It was a singular and curious malaise that had come over him, and he hardly knew what to make of it. He felt as though he were doing something that was strongly objected to by another person, another person, moreover, who had some right to object. It was a most disturbing and disagreeable feeling, not unlike the persistent promptings of conscience: almost, in fact, as if he were doing something he knew to be wrong. Yet, though he searched vigorously and honestly in his mind, he could nowhere lay his finger upon the secret of this growing uneasiness, and it perplexed him. More, it distressed and frightened him.

"Pure nerves, I suppose," he said aloud with a forced laugh. "Mountain air will cure all that! Ah," he added, still speaking to himself, "and that reminds me—my snow-glasses."

He was standing by the door of the bedroom during this brief soliloquy, and as he passed quickly toward the sitting room to fetch them from the cupboard he saw out of the corner of his eye the indistinct outline of a figure standing on the stairs, a few feet from the top. It was someone in a stooping position, with one hand on the banister, and the face peering up toward the landing. And at the same moment he heard a shuffling footstep. The person who had been creeping about below all this time had at last come up to his own floor. Who in the world could it be? And what in the name of Heaven did he want?

Johnson caught his breath sharply and stood stock still. Then, after a few seconds' hesitation, he found his courage and turned to investigate. The stairs, he saw to his utter amazement, were empty; there was no one. He felt a series of cold shivers run over him, and something about the muscles of his legs gave a little and grew weak. For the space of several minutes he peered steadily into the shadows that congregated about the top of the staircase where he had seen the figure, and then he walked fast—almost ran, in fact—into the light of the front room; but hardly had he passed inside the doorway when he heard someone come up the stairs behind him with a quick bound and go swiftly into his bedroom. It was a heavy, but at the same time a stealthy footstep—the tread of somebody who did not wish to be seen. And it was at this precise moment that the nervousness he had hitherto experienced leaped the boundary line and entered the state of fear, almost of acute, unreasoning fear. Before it turned into terror there was a further boundary to cross, and beyond that again lay the region of pure horror. Johnson's position was an unenviable one.

"By Jove! That *was* someone on the stairs, then," he muttered, his flesh crawling all over; "and whoever it was has now gone into my bedroom." His delicate, pale face turned absolutely white, and for some minutes he hardly knew what to think or do. Then he realized intuitively that delay only set a premium upon fear; and he crossed the landing boldly and went straight into the other room, where, a few seconds before, the steps had disappeared.

"Who's there? Is that you, Mrs. Monks?" he called aloud, as he went, and heard the first half of his words echo down the empty stairs, while the second half fell dead against the curtains in a room that apparently held no other human figure than his own.

"Who's there?" he called again, in a voice unnecessarily loud and that only just held firm. "What do you want here?"

The curtains swayed very slightly, and, as he saw it, his heart felt as if it almost missed a beat; yet he dashed forward and drew them aside with a rush. A window, streaming with rain, was all that met his gaze. He continued his search, but in vain; the cupboards held nothing but rows of clothes, hanging motionless; and under the bed there was no sign of anyone hiding. He stepped backward into the middle of the room, and, as he did so, something all but tripped him up. Turning with a sudden spring of alarm he saw—the kit-bag.

"Odd!" he thought. "That's not where I left it!" A few moments before it had surely been on his right, between the bed and the bath; he did not remember having moved it. It was very curious. What in the world was the matter with everything? Were all his senses gone queer? A terrific gust of wind tore at the windows, dashing the sleet against the glass with the force of a small gunshot, and then fled away howling dismally over the waste of Bloomsbury roofs. A sudden vision of the Channel next day rose in his mind and recalled him sharply to realities.

"There's no one here at any rate; that's quite clear!" he exclaimed aloud. Yet at the time he uttered them he knew perfectly well that his words were not true and that he did not believe them himself. He felt exactly as though someone was hiding close about him, watching all his movements, trying to hinder his packing in some way. "And two of my senses," he added, keeping up the pretence, "have played me the most absurd tricks: the steps I heard and the figure I saw were both entirely imaginary."

He went back to the front room, poked the fire into a blaze, and sat down before it to think. What impressed him more than anything else was the fact that the kit-bag was no longer where he had left it. It had been dragged nearer to the door.

What happened afterward that night happened, of course, to a man already excited by fear, and was perceived by a mind that had not the full and proper control, therefore, of the senses. Outwardly, Johnson remained calm and master of himself to the end, pretending to the very last that everything he witnessed had a natural explanation, or was merely delusions of his tired nerves. But inwardly, in his very heart, he knew all along that someone had been hiding downstairs in the empty suite when he came in, that this person had watched for his opportunity and then stealthily made his way up to the bedroom, and that all he saw and heard afterward, from the moving of the kit-bag to—well, to the other things this story has to tell—were caused directly by the presence of this invisible person.

And it was here, just when he most desired to keep his mind and thoughts controlled, that the vivid pictures received day after day upon the mental plates exposed in the courtroom of the Old Bailey, came strongly to light and developed themselves in the dark room of his inner vision. Unpleasant, haunting memories have a way of coming to life again just when the mind least desires them—in the silent watches of the night, on sleepless pillows, during the lonely hours spent by sick and dying beds. And so now, in the same way, Johnson saw nothing but the dreadful face of John Turk, the murderer, lowering at him from every corner of his mental field of vision; the white skin, the evil eyes, and the fringe of black hair low over the forehead. All the pictures of those ten days in court crowded back into his mind unbidden, and very vivid.

"This is all rubbish and nerves," he exclaimed at length,

springing with sudden energy from his chair. "I shall finish my packing and go to bed. I'm overwrought, overtired. No doubt, at this rate I shall hear steps and things all night!"

But his face was deadly white all the same. He snatched up his field glasses and walked across to the bedroom, humming a music hall song as he went—a trifle too loud to be natural; and the instant he crossed the threshold and stood within the room something turned cold about his heart, and he felt that every hair on his head stood up.

The kit-bag lay close in front of him, several feet nearer to the door than he had left it, and just over its crumpled top he saw a head and face slowly sinking down out of sight as though someone were crouching behind it to hide, and at the same moment a sound like a long-drawn sigh was distinctly audible in the still air about him between the gusts of the storm outside.

Johnson had more courage and willpower than the girlish indecision of his face indicated; but at first such a wave of terror came over him that for some seconds he could do nothing but stand and stare. A violent trembling ran down his back and legs, and he was conscious of a foolish, almost an hysterical, impulse to scream aloud. That sigh seemed in his very ear, and the air still quivered with it. It was unmistakably a human sigh.

"Who's there?" he said at length, finding his voice; but though he meant to speak with loud decision, the tones came out instead in a faint whisper, for he had partly lost the control of his tongue and lips.

He stepped forward, so that he could see all around and over the kit-bag. Of course there was nothing there, nothing but the faded carpet and the bulging canvas sides. He put out his hands and threw open the mouth of the sack where it had fallen over, being only three parts full, and then he saw for the first time that around the inside, some six inches from the top, there ran a broad

smear of dull crimson. It was an old and faded bloodstain. He uttered a scream, and drew back his hands as if they had been burned. At the same moment the kit-bag gave a faint, but unmistakable, lurch forward toward the door.

Johnson collapsed backward, searching with his hands for the support of something solid, and the door, being farther behind him than he realized, received his weight just in time to prevent his falling, and shut to with a resounding bang. At the same moment the swinging of his left arm accidentally touched the electric switch, and the light in the room went out.

It was an awkward and disagreeable predicament, and if Johnson had not been possessed of real pluck he might have done all manner of foolish things. As it was, however, he pulled himself together, and groped furiously for the little brass knob to turn the light on again. But the rapid closing of the door had set the coats hanging on it a-swinging, and his fingers became entangled in a confusion of sleeves and pockets, so that it was some moments before he found the switch. And in those few moments of bewilderment and terror two things happened that sent him beyond recall over the boundary into the region of genuine horror—he distinctly heard the kit-bag shuffling heavily across the floor in jerks, and close in front of his face sounded once again the sigh of a human being.

In his anguished efforts to find the brass button on the wall he nearly scraped the nails from his fingers, but even then, in those frenzied moments of alarm—so swift and alert are the impressions of a mind keyed up by a vivid emotion—he had time to realize that he dreaded the return of the light, and that it might be better for him to stay hidden in the merciful screen of darkness. It was but the impulse of a moment, however, and before he had time to act upon it he had yielded automatically to the original desire, and the room was flooded again with light.

But the second instinct had been right. It would have been better for him to have stayed in the shelter of the kind darkness. For there, close before him, bending over the half-packed kit-bag, clear as life in the merciless glare of the electric light, stood the figure of John Turk, the murderer. Not three feet from him the man stood, the fringe of black hair marked plainly against the pallor of the forehead,

the whole horrible presentment of the scoundrel, as vivid as he had seen him day after day in the Old Bailey, when he stood there in the dock, cynical and callous, under the very shadow of the gallows.

In a flash Johnson realized what it all meant: the dirty and much-used bag; the smear of crimson within the top; the dreadful stretched condition of the bulging sides. He remembered how the victim's body had been stuffed into a canvas bag for burial, the ghastly, dismembered fragments forced with lime into this very bag; and the bag itself produced as evidence—it all came back to him as clear as day ...

Very softly and stealthily his hand groped behind him for the handle of the door, but before he could actually turn it the very thing that he most of all dreaded came about, and John Turk lifted his devil's face and looked at him. At the same moment that heavy sigh passed through the air of the room, formulated somehow into words: "It's my bag. And I want it."

Johnson just remembered clawing the door open, and then falling in a heap upon the floor of the landing, as he tried frantically to make his way into the front room.

He remained unconscious for a long time, and it was still dark when he opened his eyes and realized that he was lying, stiff and bruised, on the cold boards. Then the memory of what he had seen rushed back into his mind, and he promptly fainted again. When he woke the second time the wintry dawn was just beginning to peep in at the windows, painting the stairs a cheerless, dismal gray, and he managed to crawl into the front room, and cover himself with an overcoat in the armchair, where at length he fell asleep.

A great clamor woke him. He recognized Mrs. Monks's voice, loud and voluble.

"What! You ain't been to bed, sir! Are you ill, or has anything

'appened? And there's an urgent gentleman to see you, though it ain't seven o'clock yet, and—"

"Who is it?" he stammered. "I'm all right, thanks. Fell asleep in my chair, I suppose."

"Someone from Mr. Wilb'rim's, and he says he ought to see you quick before you go abroad, and I told him—"

"Show him up, please, at once," said Johnson, whose head was whirling, and his mind was still full of dreadful visions.

Mr. Wilbraham's man came in with many apologies, and explained briefly and quickly that an absurd mistake had been made, and that the wrong kit-bag had been sent over the night before.

"Henry somehow got hold of the one that came over from the courtroom, and Mr. Wilbraham only discovered it when he saw his own lying in his room, and asked why it had not gone to you," the man said.

"Oh!" said Johnson stupidly.

"And he must have brought you the one from the murder case instead, sir, I'm afraid," the man continued, without the ghost of an expression on his face. "The one John Turk packed the dead body in. Mr. Wilbraham's awful upset about it, sir, and told me to come over first thing this morning with the right one, as you were leaving by the boat."

He pointed to a clean-looking kit-bag on the floor, which he had just brought. "And I was to bring the other one back, sir," he added casually.

For some minutes Johnson could not find his voice. At last he pointed in the direction of his bedroom. "Perhaps you would kindly unpack it for me. Just empty the things out on the floor."

The man disappeared into the other room, and was gone for five minutes. Johnson heard the shifting to and fro of the bag, and the rattle of the skates and boots being unpacked.

"Thank you, sir," the man said, returning with the bag folded over his arm. "And can I do anything more to help you, sir?"

"What is it?" asked Johnson, seeing that he still had something he wished to say.

The man shuffled and looked mysterious. "Beg pardon, sir, but knowing your interest in the Turk case, I thought you'd maybe like to know what's happened—"

"Yes."

"John Turk killed himself last night with poison immediately on getting his release, and he left a note for Mr. Wilbraham saying as he'd be much obliged if they'd have him put away, same as the woman he murdered, in the old kit-bag."

"What time—did he do it?" asked Johnson.

"Ten o'clock last night, sir, the warder says."

The Pocket

SEAN O'HUIGIN

i reached
into my
pocket
and much
to my
surprise
something in
there
grabbed me
and pulled
me right
inside
i felt
its clammy
fingers
all bony
cold and
thin
i tried to
keep my
head out
no use

it all
went in
and that
was not
the end
of it
the pocket
seemed
so deep
and dark
and strange
and scary
i felt i
had to
weep
"shut up
you silly
creature"
a voice
yelled
in my
ear
and then
my feet
were
pulled inside
and i had
disappeared

The Story-Teller

SAKI

It was a hot afternoon, and the railway carriage was correspondingly sultry, and the next stop was at Templecombe, nearly an hour ahead. The occupants of the carriage were a small girl, and a smaller girl, and a small boy. An aunt belonging to the children occupied one corner seat, and the further corner seat on the opposite side was occupied by a bachelor who was a stranger to their party, but the small girls and the small boy emphatically occupied the compartment. Both the aunt and the children were conversational in a limited, persistent way, reminding one of the attentions of a housefly that refused to be discouraged. Most of the aunt's remarks seemed to begin with "Don't," and nearly all of the children's remarks began with "Why?" The bachelor said nothing out loud.

"Don't, Cyril, don't," exclaimed the aunt, as the small boy began smacking the cushions of the seat, producing a cloud of dust at each blow.

"Come and look out of the window," she added.

The child moved reluctantly to the window. "Why are those sheep being driven out of that field?" he asked.

"I expect they are being driven to another field where there is more grass," said the aunt weakly.

"But there is lots of grass in that field," protested the boy. "There's nothing else but grass there. Aunt, there's lots of grass in that field."

"Perhaps the grass in the other field is better," suggested the aunt fatuously.

"Why is it better?" came the swift, inevitable question.

"Oh, look at those cows!" exclaimed the aunt. Nearly every field along the line had contained cows or bullocks, but she spoke as though she were drawing attention to a rarity.

"Why is the grass in the other field better?" persisted Cyril.

The frown on the bachelor's face was deepening to a scowl. He was a hard, unsympathetic man, the aunt decided in her mind. She was utterly unable to come to any satisfactory decision about the grass in the other field.

The smaller girl created a diversion by beginning to recite "On the Road to Mandalay." She only knew the first line, but she put her limited knowledge to the fullest possible use. She repeated the line over and over again in a dreamy but resolute and very audible voice; it seemed to the bachelor as though someone had had a bet with her that she could not repeat the line aloud two thousand times without stopping. Whoever it was who had made the wager was likely to lose his bet.

"Come over here and listen to a story," said the aunt, when the bachelor had looked twice at her and once at the communication cord.

The children moved listlessly toward the aunt's end of the carriage. Evidently her reputation as a story-teller did not rank high in their estimation.

In a low, confidential voice, interrupted at frequent intervals by loud, petulant questions from her listeners, she began an unenterprising and deplorably uninteresting story about a little girl who was good, and made friends with every one on account of her goodness, and was finally saved from a mad bull by a number of rescuers who admired her moral character.

"Wouldn't they have saved her if she hadn't been good?" demanded the bigger of the small girls. It was exactly the question that the bachelor had wanted to ask.

"Well, yes," admitted the aunt lamely, "but I don't think they would have run quite so fast to her help if they had not liked her so much."

"It's the stupidest story I've ever heard," said the bigger of the small girls, with immense conviction.

"I didn't listen after the first bit, it was so stupid," said Cyril.

The smaller girl made no actual comment on the story, but she had long ago recommenced a murmured repetition of her favorite line.

"You don't seem to be a success as a story-teller," said the bachelor suddenly from his corner.

The aunt bristled in instant defence at this unexpected attack.

"It's a very difficult thing to tell stories that children can both understand and appreciate," she said stiffly.

"I don't agree with you," said the bachelor.

"Perhaps *you* would like to tell them a story," was the aunt's retort.

"Tell us a story," demanded the bigger of the small girls.

"Once upon a time," began the bachelor, "there was a little girl called Bertha, who was extraordinarily good."

The children's momentarily aroused interest began at once to flicker; all stories seemed dreadfully alike, no matter who told them.

"She did all that she was told, she was always truthful, she kept her clothes clean, ate milk puddings as though they were jam tarts, learned her lessons perfectly, and was polite in her manners."

"Was she pretty?" asked the bigger of the small girls.

"Not as pretty as any of you," said the bachelor, "but she was horribly good."

There was a wave of reaction in favor of the story; the word horrible in connection with goodness was a novelty that commended itself. It seemed to introduce a ring of truth that was absent from the aunt's tales of infant life.

"She was so good," continued the bachelor, "that she won several medals for goodness, which she always wore, pinned on to her dress. There was a medal for obedience, another medal for

punctuality, and a third for good behavior. They were large metal medals and they clicked against one another as she walked. No other child in the town where she lived had as many as three medals, so everybody knew that she must be an extra good child."

"Horribly good," quoted Cyril.

"Everybody talked about her goodness, and the Prince of the country got to hear about it, and he said that as she was so very good she might be allowed once a week to walk in his park, which was just outside the town. It was a beautiful park, and no children were ever allowed in it, so it was a great honor for Bertha to be allowed to go there."

"Were there any sheep in the park?" demanded Cyril.

"No," said the bachelor, "there were no sheep."

"Why weren't there any sheep?" came the inevitable question arising out of that answer.

The aunt permitted herself a smile, which might almost have been described as a grin.

"There were no sheep in the park," said the bachelor, "because the Prince's mother had once had a dream that her son would either be killed by a sheep or else by a clock falling on him. For that reason the Prince never kept a sheep in his park or a clock in his palace."

The aunt suppressed a gasp of admiration.

"Was the Prince killed by a sheep or by a clock?" asked Cyril.

"He is still alive, so we can't tell whether the dream will come true," said the bachelor unconcernedly. "Anyway, there were no sheep in the park, but there were lots of little pigs running all over the place."

"What color were they?"

"Black with white faces, white with black spots, black all over, grey with white patches, and some were white all over."

The story-teller paused to let a full idea of the park's treasures sink into the children's imaginations; then he resumed:

"Bertha was rather sorry to find that there were no flowers in the park. She had promised her aunts, with tears in her eyes, that she would not pick any of the kind Prince's flowers, and she had meant to keep her promise, so of course it made her feel silly to find that there were no flowers to pick."

"Why weren't there any flowers?"

"Because the pigs had eaten them all," said the bachelor promptly. "The gardeners had told the Prince that you couldn't have pigs and flowers, so he decided to have pigs and no flowers."

There was a murmur of approval at the excellence of the Prince's decision; so many people would have decided the other way.

"There were lots of other delightful things in the park. There were ponds with gold and blue and green fish in them, and trees with beautiful parrots that said clever things at a moment's notice, and humming birds that hummed all the popular tunes of the day. Bertha walked up and down and enjoyed herself immensely, and thought to herself: 'If I were not so extraordinarily good I should not have been allowed to come into this beautiful park and enjoy all that there is to be seen in it,' and her three medals clinked against one another as she walked and helped to remind her how very good she really was. Just then an enormous wolf came prowling into the park to see if it could catch a fat little pig for its supper."

"What color was it?" asked the children, amid an immediate quickening of interest.

"Mud-color all over, with a black tongue and pale gray eyes that gleamed with unspeakable ferocity. The first thing that it saw in the park was Bertha; her pinafore was so spotlessly white and clean that it could be seen from a great distance. Bertha saw the wolf and saw that it was stealing toward her, and she began to wish that she had never been allowed to come into the park. She ran as hard as she could, and the wolf came after her with huge leaps and bounds. She managed to reach a shrubbery of myrtle bushes and she hid herself in one of the thickest of the bushes. The wolf came sniffing among the branches, its black tongue lolling out of its mouth and its pale gray eyes glaring with rage. Bertha was terribly frightened, and thought to herself: 'If I had not been so extraordinarily good I should have been safe in the town at this moment.' However, the scent of the myrtle was so strong that the wolf could not sniff out where Bertha was hiding, and the bushes were so thick that he might have hunted about in them for a long time without catching sight of her, so he thought he might as well go off and catch a little pig instead. Bertha was trembling very much at having the wolf prowling and sniffing so near her, and as she trembled the medal for obedience clinked against the medals for good conduct and punctuality. The wolf was just moving away when he heard the sound of the medals clinking and stopped to listen; they clinked again in a bush quite near him. He dashed into the bush, his pale gray eyes gleaming with ferocity and triumph, and dragged Bertha out and devoured her to the last morsel. All that was left of her were her shoes, bits of clothing, and the three medals for goodness."

"Were any of the little pigs killed?"

"No, they all escaped."

"The story began badly," said the smaller of the small girls, "but it had a beautiful ending."

"It is the most beautiful story that I ever heard," said the bigger of the small girls, with immense decision.

"It is the *only* beautiful story I have ever heard," said Cyril.

A dissentient opinion came from the aunt.

"A most improper story to tell to young children! You have undermined the effect of years of careful teaching."

"At any rate," said the bachelor, collecting his belongings preparatory to leaving the carriage, "I kept them quiet for ten minutes, which was more than you were able to do."

"Unhappy woman!" he observed to himself as he walked down the platform of Templecombe station. "For the next six months or so those children will assail her in public with demands for an improper story!"

John Charrington's Wedding

E. NESBIT

No one ever thought that May Forster would marry John Charrington; but he thought differently, and things which John Charrington intended had a queer way of coming to pass. He asked her to marry him before he went up to Oxford. She laughed and refused him. He asked her again next time he came home. Again she laughed, tossed her dainty blonde head, and again refused. A third time he asked her; she said it was becoming a confirmed bad habit, and laughed at him more than ever.

John was not the only man who wanted to marry her: she was the belle of our village coterie, and we were all in love with her more or less; it was a sort of fashion, like heliotrope ties or Inverness capes. Therefore we were as much annoyed as surprised when John Charrington walked into our little local Club—we held it in a loft over the saddler's, I remember—and invited us all to his wedding.

"Your wedding?"

"You don't mean it?"

"Who's the happy pair? When's it to be?"

John Charrington filled his pipe and lighted it before he replied. Then he said:

"I'm sorry to deprive you fellows of your only joke—but Miss Forster and I are to be married in September."

"You don't mean it?"

"He's got the mitten again, and it's turned his head."

"No," I said, rising, "I see it's true. Lend me a pistol, someone—or a first-class fare to the other end of Nowhere. Charrington has bewitched the only pretty girl in our twenty-mile radius. Was it mesmerism, or a love-potion, Jack?"

"Neither, sir, but a gift you'll never have—perseverance—and the best luck a man ever had in this world."

There was something in his voice that silenced me, and all chaff of the other fellows failed to draw him further.

The queer thing about it was that when we congratulated Miss Forster, she blushed and smiled and dimpled, for all the world as though she were in love with him, and had been in love with him all the time. Upon my word, I think she had. Women are strange creatures.

We were all asked to the wedding. In Brixham everyone who was anybody knew everybody else who was anyone. My sisters were, I truly believe, more interested in the *trousseau* than the bride herself, and I was to be best man. The coming marriage was much canvassed at afternoon tea-tables, and at our little Club over the saddler's, and the question was always asked. "Does she care for him?"

I used to ask that question myself in the early days of their engagement, but after a certain evening in August I never asked it again. I was coming home from the Club through the churchyard. Our church is on a thyme-grown hill, and the turf about it is so thick and soft that one's footsteps are noiseless.

I made no sound as I vaulted the low lichened wall, and threaded my way between the tombstones. It was at the same instant that I heard John Charrington's voice, and saw Her. May was sitting on a low flat gravestone, her face turned toward the full splendor of the western sun. Its expression ended, at once and for ever, any question of love for him; it was transfigured to a beauty I should not have believed possible, even to that beautiful little face.

John lay at her feet, and it was his voice that broke the stillness of the golden August evening.

"My dear, my dear, I believe I should come back from the dead if you wanted me!"

I coughed at once to indicate my presence, and passed on into the shadow fully enlightened.

The wedding was to be early in September. Two days before I had to run up to town on business. The train was late, of course, for we are on the South-Eastern, and as I stood grumbling with my watch in my hand, whom should I see but John Charrington and May Forster. They were walking up and down the unfrequented end of the platform, arm in arm, looking into each other's eyes, careless of the sympathetic interest of the porters.

Of course I knew better than to hesitate a moment before burying myself in the booking-office, and it was not till the train drew up at the platform, that I obtrusively passed the pair with my Gladstone, and took the corner in a first-class smoking-

carriage. I did this with as good an air of not seeing them as I could assume. I pride myself on my discretion, but if John were traveling alone I wanted his company. I had it.

"Hullo, old man," came his cheery voice as he swung his bag into my carriage. "Here's luck; I was expecting a dull journey!"

"Where are you off to?" I asked, discretion still bidding me turn my eyes away, though I saw, without looking, that hers were red-rimmed.

"To old Branbridge's," he answered, shutting the door and leaning out for a last word with his sweetheart.

"Oh, I wish you wouldn't go, John," she was saying in a low, earnest voice. "I feel certain something will happen."

"Do you think I should let anything happen to keep me, and the day after tomorrow our wedding-day?"

"Don't go," she answered, with a pleading intensity which would have sent my Gladstone on to the platform and me after it. But she wasn't speaking to me. John Charrington was made differently; he rarely changed his opinions, never his resolutions.

He only stroked the little ungloved hands that lay on the carriage door.

"I must, May. The old boy's been awfully good to me, and now he's dying I must go and see him, but I shall come home in time for—" the rest of the parting was lost in a whisper and in the rattling lurch of the starting train.

"You're sure to come?" she spoke as the train moved.

"Nothing shall keep me," he answered; and we steamed out. After he had seen the last of the little figure on the platform he leaned back in his corner and kept silence for a minute.

When he spoke, it was to explain to me that his godfather, whose heir he was, lay dying at Peasmarsh Place, some fifty miles away, and had sent for John, and John had felt bound to go.

"I shall be surely back tomorrow," he said, "or, if not, the day after, in heaps of time. Thank Heaven, one hasn't to get up in the middle of the night to get married nowadays!"

"And suppose Mr. Branbridge dies?"

"Alive or dead I mean to be married on Thursday!" John answered, lighting a cigar and unfolding *The Times*.

At Peasmarsh station we said "good-bye," and he got out, and I saw him ride off. I went on to London, where I stayed the night.

When I got home the next afternoon, a very wet one, by the way, my sister greeted me with:

"Where's Mr. Charrington?"

"Goodness knows," I answered testily. Every man, since Cain, has resented that kind of question.

"I thought you might have heard from him," she went on, "as you're to give him away tomorrow."

"Isn't he back?" I asked, for I had confidently expected to find him at home.

"No, Geoffrey,"—my sister Fanny always had a way of jumping to conclusions, especially such conclusions as were least favorable to her fellow-creatures—"he has not returned, and, what is more, you may depend upon it he won't. You mark my words, there'll be no wedding tomorrow."

My sister Fanny has a power of annoying me which no other human being possesses.

"You mark my words," I retorted with asperity, "you had better give up making such a thundering idiot of yourself. There'll be more wedding tomorrow than ever you'll take the first part in." A prophecy which, by the way, came true.

But though I could snarl confidently to my sister, I did not feel so comfortable when late that night, I, standing on the doorstep of John's house, heard that he had not returned. I went home gloomily through the rain. Next morning brought a brilliant blue sky, gold sun, and all such softness of air and beauty of cloud as go to make up a perfect day. I woke with a vague feeling of having gone to bed anxious, and of being rather averse to facing that anxiety in the light of full wakefulness.

But with my shaving-water came a note from John which relieved my mind and sent me up to the Forsters with a light heart.

May was in the garden. I saw her blue gown through the hollyhocks as the lodge gates swung to behind me. So I did not go up to the house, but turned aside down the turfed path.

"He's written to you too," she said, without preliminary greeting, when I reached her side.

"Yes, I'm to meet him at the station at three, and come straight on to the church."

Her face looked pale, but there was a brightness in her eyes, and a tender quiver about the mouth that spoke of renewed happiness.

"Mr. Branbridge begged him so to stay another night that he had not the heart to refuse," she went on. "He is so kind, but I wish he hadn't stayed."

I was at the station at half-past two. I felt rather annoyed with John. It seemed a sort of slight to the beautiful girl who loved him, that he should come as it were out of breath, and with the dust of travel upon him, to take her hand, which some of us would have given the best years of our lives to take.

But when the three o'clock train glided in, and glided out again having brought no passengers to our little station, I was more than annoyed. There was no other train for thirty-five minutes; I calculated that, with much hurry, we might just get to the church in time for the ceremony; but, oh, what a fool to miss that first train! What other man could have done it?

That thirty-five minutes seemed a year, as I wandered round

the station reading the advertisements and the timetables, and the company's bylaws, and getting more and more angry with John Charrington. This confidence in his own power of getting everything he wanted the minute he wanted it was leading him too far. I hate waiting. Everyone does, but I believe I hate it more than anyone else. The three-thirty-five was late, of course.

I ground my pipe between my teeth and stamped with impatience as I watched the signals. Click. The signal went down. Five minutes later I flung myself into the carriage that I had brought for John.

"Drive to the church!" I said, as someone shut the door. "Mr. Charrington hasn't come by this train."

Anxiety now replaced anger. What had become of the man? Could he have been taken suddenly ill? I had never known him have a day's illness in his life. And even so he might have telegraphed. Some awful accident must have happened to him. The thought that he had played her false never—no, not for a moment—entered my head. Yes, something terrible had happened to him, and on me lay the task of telling his bride. I almost wished the carriage would upset and break my head so that someone else might tell her, not I, who—but that's nothing to do with this story.

It was five minutes to four as we drew up at the churchyard gate. A double row of eager onlookers lined the path from lychgate to porch. I sprang from the carriage and passed up between them. Our gardener had a good front place near the door. I stopped.

"Are they waiting still, Byles?" I asked, simply to gain time, for of course I knew they were by the waiting crowd's attentive attitude.

"Waiting, sir? No, no, sir; why, it must be over by now."

"Over! Then Mr. Charrington's come?"

"To the minute, sir; must have missed you somehow, and I say, sir," lowering his voice, "I never see Mr. John the least bit so afore, but my opinion is he's been drinking pretty free. His clothes was

all dusty and his face like a sheet. I tell you I didn't like the looks of him at all, and the folks inside are saying all sorts of things. You'll see, something's gone very wrong with Mr. John, and he's tried liquor. He looked like a ghost, and in he went with his eyes straight before him, with never a look or a word for none of us: him that was always such a gentleman!"

I had never heard Byles make so long a speech. The crowd in the churchyard were talking in whispers and getting ready rice and slippers to throw at the bride and bridegroom. The ringers were ready with their hands on the ropes to ring out the merry peal as the bride and bridegroom should come out.

A murmur from the church announced them; out they came. Byles was right. John Charrington did not look himself. There was dust on his coat, his hair was disarranged. He seemed to have been in some row, for there was a black mark above his eyebrow. He was deathly pale. But his pallor was not greater than that of the

bride, who might have been carved in ivory—dress, veil, orange blossoms, face and all.

As they passed out the ringers stooped—there were six of them—and then, on the ears expecting the gay wedding peal, came the slow tolling of the passing bell.

A thrill of horror at so foolish a jest from the ringers passed through us all. But the ringers themselves dropped the ropes and fled like rabbits out into the sunlight. The bride shuddered, and gray shadows came about her mouth, but the bridegroom led her on down the path where the people stood with the handfuls of rice; but the handfuls were never thrown, and the wedding-bells never rang. In vain the ringers were urged to remedy their mistake: they protested with many whispered expletives that they would see themselves further first.

In a hush like the hush in the chamber of death the bridal pair passed into their carriage and its door slammed behind them.

Then the tongues were loosed. A babel of anger, wonder, conjecture from the guests and the spectators.

"If I'd seen his condition, sir," said old Forster to me as we drove off, "I would have stretched him on the floor of the church, sir, by Heaven I would, before I'd have let him marry my daughter!"

Then he put his head out of the window.

"Drive like hell," he cried to the coachman; "don't spare the horses."

He was obeyed. We passed the bride's carriage. I forbore to look at it, and old Forster turned his head away and swore. We reached home before it.

We stood in the hall doorway, in the blazing afternoon sun, and in about half a minute we heard wheels crunching the gravel. When the carriage stopped in front of the steps old Forster and I ran down.

"Great Heaven, the carriage is empty! And yet—"

I had the door open in a minute, and this is what I saw …

No sign of John Charrington; and of May, his wife, only a huddled heap of white satin lying half on the floor of the carriage and half on the seat.

"I drove straight here, sir," said the coachman, as the bride's father lifted her out; "and I'll swear no one got out of the carriage."

We carried her into the house in her bridal dress and drew back her veil. I saw her face. Shall I ever forget it? White, white and drawn with agony and horror, bearing such a look of terror as I have never seen since except in dreams. And her hair, her radiant blonde hair, I tell you it was white like snow.

As we stood, her father and I, half mad with the horror and mystery of it, a boy came up the avenue—a telegraph boy. They brought the orange envelope to me. I tore it open.

Mr. Charrington was thrown from the dogcart on his way to the station at half-past one. Killed on the spot!

And he was married to May Forster in our parish church at *half-past three*, in presence of half the parish.

"I shall be married, dead or alive!"

What had passed in that carriage on the homeward drive? No one knows—no one will ever know. Oh, May! Oh, my dear!

Before a week was over they laid her beside her husband in our little churchyard on the thyme-covered hill—the churchyard where they had kept their love-trysts.

Thus was accomplished John Charrington's wedding.

The Voice in the Night

WILLIAM HOPE HODGSON

It was a dark, starless night. We were becalmed in the Northern Pacific. Our exact position I do not know; for the sun had been hidden, during the course of a weary, breathless week, by a thin haze which had seemed to float above us, about the height of our mastheads, at whiles descending and shrouding the surrounding sea.

With there being no wind, we had steadied the tiller, and I was the only man on deck. The crew, consisting of two men and a boy, were sleeping forward in their den; while Will—my friend, and the master of our little craft—was aft in his bunk on the port side of the little cabin.

Suddenly, from out of the surrounding darkness, there came a hail: "Schooner, ahoy!"

The cry was so unexpected that I gave no immediate answer, because of my surprise.

It came again—a voice curiously throaty and inhuman, calling from somewhere upon the dark sea away on our port broadside.

"Schooner, ahoy!"

"Hullo!" I sang out, having gathered my wits somewhat. "What are you? What do you want?"

"You need not be afraid," answered the queer voice, having probably noticed some trace of confusion in my tone. "I am only an old—man."

The pause sounded oddly; but it was only afterward that it came back to me with any significance.

"Why don't you come alongside, then?" I queried somewhat snappishly; for I liked not his hinting at my having been a trifle shaken.

"I—I—can't. It wouldn't be safe. I—" The voice broke off, and there was silence.

"What do you mean?" I asked, growing more and more astonished. "What would not be safe? Where are you?"

I listened for a moment; but there came no answer. And then, a sudden indefinite suspicion of I knew not what coming to me, I stepped swiftly to the binnacle, and took out the lighted lamp. At the same time, I knocked on the deck with my heel to waken Will. Then I was back at the side, throwing the yellow funnel of light out into the silent immensity beyond our rail. As I did so, I heard a slight, muffled cry, and then the sound of a splash as though someone had dipped oars abruptly. Yet I cannot say that I saw anything with certainty; save, it seemed to me, that in the first flash of the light, there had been something upon the waters, where now there was nothing.

"Hullo, there!" I called. "What foolery is this!"

But there came only the indistinct sounds of a boat being pulled away into the night.

Then I heard Will's voice, from the direction of the after scuttle.

"What's up, George?"

"Come here, Will!" I said.

"What is it?" he asked, coming across the deck.

I told him the queer thing which had happened. He put several questions; then, after a moment's silence, he raised his hands to his lips and hailed, "Boat, ahoy!"

From a long distance away there came back to us a faint reply, and my companion repeated his call. Presently, after a short period of silence, there grew on our hearing the muffled sound of oars; at which Will hailed again.

This time there was a reply. "Put away the light."

Will told me to do as the voice bade, and I shoved it down under the bulwarks.

"Come nearer," he said, and the oar strokes continued. Then, when apparently some half-dozen fathoms distant, they again ceased.

"Come alongside," exclaimed Will. "There's nothing to be frightened of aboard here!"

"Promise that you will not show the light?"

"What's to do with you," I burst out, "that you're so infernally afraid of the light?"

"Because—" began the voice, and stopped short.

"Because what?" I asked quickly.

Will put his hand on my shoulder. "Shut up a minute, old man," he said in a low voice. "Let me tackle him."

He leaned more over the rail.

"See here, mister," he said, "this is a pretty queer business, you coming upon us like this, right out in the middle of the blessed Pacific. How are we to know what sort of a hanky-panky trick you're up to? You say there's only one of you. How are we to know, unless we get a squint at you—eh? What's your objection to the light, anyway?"

As he finished, I heard the noise of the oars again, and then the voice came; but now from a greater distance, and sounding extremely hopeless and pathetic.

"I am sorry—sorry! I would not have troubled you, only I am hungry, and—so is she."

The voice died away, and the sound of the oars, dipping irregularly, was borne to us.

"Stop!" sang out Will. "I don't want to drive you away. Come back! We'll keep the light hidden, if you don't like it."

He turned to me. "It's a queer rig, this; but I think there's nothing to be afraid of?"

There was a question in his tone, and I replied. "No, I think the poor devil's been wrecked around here, and gone crazy."

The sound of the oars drew nearer.

"Shove that lamp back in the binnacle," said Will; then he leaned over the rail and listened. I replaced the lamp, and came back to his side. The dipping of the oars ceased some dozen yards distant.

"Won't you come alongside now?" asked Will in an even voice. "I have had the lamp put back in the binnacle."

"I—I cannot," replied the voice. "I dare not come nearer. I dare not even pay you for the—the provisions."

"That's all right," said Will, and hesitated. "You're welcome to as much grub as you can take—" Again he hesitated.

"You are very good," exclaimed the voice. "May God, Who understands everything, reward you—" It broke off huskily.

"The—the lady?" said Will abruptly. "Is she—"

"I have left her behind upon the island," came the voice.

"What island?" I cut in.

"I know not its name," returned the voice. "I would to God—!" it began, and checked itself as suddenly.

"Could we not send a boat for her?" asked Will at this point.

"No!" said the voice, with extraordinary emphasis. "My God! No!" There was a moment's pause; then it added, in a tone which seemed a merited reproach, "It was because of our want I ventured—because her agony tortured me."

"I am a forgetful brute," exclaimed Will. "Just wait a minute, whoever you are, and I will bring you up something at once."

In a couple of minutes he was back again, and his arms were full of various edibles. He paused at the rail.

"Can't you come alongside for them?" he asked.

"No—I *dare not*," replied the voice, and it seemed to me that in its tones I detected a note of stifled craving—as though the owner hushed a mortal desire. It came to me then in a flash that the poor old creature out there in the darkness was *suffering* for actual need of that which Will held in his arms; and yet, because of some unintelligible dread, refraining from dashing to the side of our schooner and receiving it. And with the lightninglike conviction, there came the knowledge that the Invisible was not mad, but sanely facing some intolerable horror.

"Will!" I said, full of many feelings, over which predominated a vast sympathy. "Get a box. We must float off the stuff to him in it."

This we did—propelling it away from the vessel, out into the darkness, by means of a boat hook. In a minute, a slight cry from the Invisible came to us, and we knew that he had secured the box.

A little later he called out a farewell to us, and so heartful a blessing that I am sure we were the better for it. Then, without more ado, we heard the ply of oars across the darkness.

"Pretty soon off," remarked Will, with perhaps just a little sense of injury.

"Wait," I replied. "I think somehow he'll come back. He must have been badly needing that food."

"And the lady," said Will. For a moment he was silent; then he continued, "It's the queerest thing ever I've stumbled across since I've been fishing."

"Yes," I said, and fell to pondering.

And so the time slipped away—an hour, another, and still Will stayed with me; for the queer adventure had knocked all desire for sleep out of him.

The third hour was three parts through when we heard again the sound of oars across the silent ocean.

"Listen!" said Will, a low note of excitement in his voice.

"He's coming, just as I thought," I muttered.

The dipping of the oars grew nearer, and I noted that the strokes were firmer and longer. The food had been needed.

They came to a stop a little distance off the broadside, and the queer voice came again to us through the darkness.

"Schooner, ahoy!"

"That you?" asked Will.

"Yes," replied the voice. "I left you suddenly; but—but there was great need."

"The lady?" questioned Will.

"The—lady is grateful now on earth. She will be more grateful soon in—in heaven."

Will began to make some reply in a puzzled voice, but became confused, and broke off short. I said nothing. I was wondering at the curious pauses, and, apart from my wonder, I was full of a great sympathy.

The voice continued. "We—she and I, have talked, as we shared the result of God's tenderness and yours—"

Will interposed; but without coherence.

"I beg of you not to—to belittle your deed of Christian charity this night," said the voice. "Be sure that it has not escaped His notice."

It stopped, and there was a full minute's silence. Then it came again.

"We have spoken together upon that which—which has befallen us. We had thought to go out, without telling anybody of the terror which has come into our—lives. She is with me in believing that tonight's happenings are under a special ruling, and that it is God's wish that we should tell to you all that we have suffered since—since—"

"Yes?" said Will softly.

"Since the sinking of the *Albatross*."

"Ah!" I exclaimed involuntarily. "She left Newcastle for 'Frisco some six months ago, and hasn't been heard of since."

"Yes," answered the voice. "But some few degrees to the north of the line she was caught in a terrible storm, and dismasted. When the day came, it was found that she was leaking badly, and presently, it falling to a calm, the sailors took to the boats, leaving—leaving a young lady—my fiancée—and myself upon the wreck.

"We were below, gathering together a few of our belongings, when they left. They were entirely callous, through fear, and when we came up on the decks, we saw them only as small shapes afar off upon the horizon. Yet we did not despair, but set to work and constructed a small raft. Upon this we put such few matters as it would hold, including a quantity of water and some ship's biscuit. Then, the vessel being very deep in the water, we got ourselves on to the raft, and pushed off.

"It was later when I observed that we seemed to be in the way of some tide or current which bore us from the ship at an angle; so that in the course of three hours, by my watch, her hull became invisible to our sight, her broken masts remaining in view for a

somewhat longer period. Then, toward evening, it grew misty, and so through the night. The next day we were still encompassed by the mist, the weather remaining quiet.

"For four days we drifted through this strange haze, until, on the evening of the fourth day, there grew upon our ears the murmur of breakers at a distance. Gradually it became plainer, and, somewhat after midnight, it appeared to sound upon either hand at no very great space. The raft was raised upon a swell several times, and then we were in smooth water, and the noise of the breakers was behind.

"When the morning came, we found that we were in a sort of great lagoon; but of this we noticed little at the time; for close before us, through the enshrouding mist, loomed the hull of a large sailing vessel. With one accord, we fell upon our knees and thanked God; for we thought that here was an end to our perils. We had much to learn.

"The raft drew near to the ship, and we shouted at them to take us aboard; but none answered. Presently the raft touched against the side of the vessel, and, seeing a rope hanging downward, I seized it and began to climb. Yet I had much ado to make my way up, because of a kind of gray, lichenous fungus which had seized upon the rope, and which blotched the side of the ship lividly.

"I reached the rail and clambered over it, on to the deck. Here I saw that the decks were covered, in great patches, with the gray masses, some of them rising into nodules several feet in height; but at the time I thought less of this matter than of the possibility of there being people aboard the ship. I shouted; but none answered. Then I went to the door below the poop deck. I opened it, and peered in. There was a great smell of staleness, so that I knew in a moment that nothing living was within, and with the knowledge, I shut the door quickly; for I felt suddenly lonely.

"I went back to the side where I had scrambled up. My—my sweetheart was still sitting quietly upon the raft. Seeing me look down, she called up to know whether there were any people aboard the ship. I replied that the vessel had the appearance of having been long deserted; but that if she would wait a little I would see whether there was anything in the shape of a ladder by which she could ascend to the deck. Then we would make a search through the vessel together. A little later, on the opposite side of the decks, I found a rope side ladder. This I carried across, and a minute afterward she was beside me.

"Together we explored the cabins and apartments in the after part of the ship; but nowhere was there any sign of life. Here and there, within the cabins themselves, we came across odd patches of that queer fungus; but this, as my sweetheart said, could be cleansed away.

"In the end, having assured ourselves that the after portion of the vessel was empty, we picked our way to the bows, between the ugly

gray nodules of that strange growth; and here we made a search, which told us that there was indeed none aboard but ourselves.

"This being now beyond any doubt, we returned to the stern of the ship and proceeded to make ourselves as comfortable as possible. Together we cleared out and cleaned two of the cabins; and after that I made examination whether there was anything eatable in the ship. This I soon found was so, and thanked God in my heart for His goodness. In addition to this I discovered the whereabouts of the fresh-water pump, and having fixed it I found the water drinkable, though somewhat unpleasant to the taste.

"For several days we stayed aboard the ship, without attempting to get to the shore. We were busily engaged in making the place habitable. Yet even thus early we became aware that our lot was even less to be desired than might have been imagined; for though, as a first step, we scraped away the odd patches of growth that studded the floors and walls of the cabins and saloon, they returned almost to their original size within the space of twenty-four hours, which not only discouraged us, but gave us a feeling of vague unease.

"Still we would not admit ourselves beaten, so set to work afresh, and not only scraped away the fungus, but soaked the places where it had been, with carbolic, a canful of which I had found in the pantry. Yet, by the end of the week the growth had returned in full strength, and, in addition it had spread to other places, as though our touching it had allowed germs from it to travel elsewhere.

"On the seventh morning, my sweetheart woke to find a small patch of it growing on her pillow, close to her face. At that, she came to me, as soon as she could get her garments upon her. I was in the galley at the time lighting the fire for breakfast.

"'Come here, John,' she said, and led me aft. When I saw the thing upon her pillow I shuddered, and then and there we agreed to go right out of the ship and see whether we could not fare to make ourselves more comfortable ashore.

"Hurriedly we gathered together our few belongings, and even among these I found that the fungus had been at work; for one of her shawls had a little lump of it growing near one edge. I threw the whole thing over the side, without saying anything to her.

"The raft was still alongside, but it was too clumsy to guide, and I lowered down a small boat that hung across the stern, and in this we made our way to the shore. Yet, as we drew near to it, I became gradually aware that here the vile fungus, which had driven us from the ship, was growing riot. In places it rose into horrible, fantastic mounds, which seemed almost to quiver, as with a quiet life, when the wind blew across them. Here and there it took on the forms of vast fingers, and in others it just spread out flat and smooth and treacherous. Odd places, it appeared as grotesque stunted trees, seeming extraordinarily kinked and gnarled—the whole quaking vilely at times.

"At first, it seemed to us that there was no single portion of the surrounding shore which was not hidden beneath the masses of the hideous lichen; yet, in this, I found we were mistaken; for somewhat later, coasting along the shore at a little distance, we descried a smooth white patch of what appeared to be fine sand, and there we landed. It was not sand. What it was I do not know. All that I have observed is that upon it the fungus will not grow; while everywhere else, save where the sandlike earth wanders oddly, pathwise, amid the gray desolation of the lichen, there is nothing but that loathsome grayness.

"It is difficult to make you understand how cheered we were to find one place that was absolutely free from the growth, and here we deposited our belongings. Then we went back to the ship for such things as it seemed to us we should need. Among other matters, I managed to bring ashore with me one of the ship's sails, with which I constructed two small tents. Though exceedingly rough shaped, they served the purposes for which they were intended. In these we lived and stored our various necessities, and thus for a matter of some four weeks all went smoothly and without particular unhappiness. Indeed, I may say with much of happiness—for—we were together.

"It was on the thumb of her right hand that the growth first showed. It was only a small circular spot, much like a little gray mole. My God! how the fear leaped to my heart when she showed me the place. We cleansed it, between us, washing it with carbolic and water. In the morning of the following day she showed her hand to me again. The gray warty thing had returned. For a little while, we looked at one another in silence. Then, still wordless, we started again to remove it. In the midst of the operation she spoke suddenly.

"'What's that on the side of your face, dear?' Her voice was sharp with anxiety. I put my hand up to feel.

"'There! Under the hair by your ear. A little to the front a bit.' My finger rested upon the place, and then I knew.

"'Let us get your thumb done first,' I said. And she submitted, only because she was afraid to touch me until it was cleansed. I finished washing and disinfecting her thumb, and then she turned to my face. After it was finished we sat together and talked awhile of many things; for there had come into our lives sudden, very terrible thoughts. We were, all at once, afraid of something worse than death. We spoke of loading the boat with provisions and water and making our way out onto the sea; yet we were helpless, for many causes, and—and the growth had attacked us already. We decided to stay. God would do with us what was His will. We would wait.

"A month, two months, three months passed, and the places grew somewhat, and there had come others. Yet we fought so strenuously with the fear that its headway was but slow, comparatively speaking.

"Occasionally we ventured off to the ship for such stores as we needed. There we found that the fungus grew persistently. One of the nodules on the main deck became soon as high as my head.

"We had now given up all thought or hope of leaving the island. We had realized that it would be unallowable to go among healthy humans, with the thing from which we were suffering.

"With this determination and knowledge in our minds we knew that we should have to husband our food and water; for we did not know, at that time, but that we should possibly live for many years.

"This reminds me that I have told you that I am an old man. Judged by years this is not so. But—but—"

He broke off; then continued somewhat abruptly.

"As I was saying, we knew that we should have to use care in the matter of food. But we had no idea then how little food there was left, of which to take care. It was a week later that I made the discovery that all the other bread tanks—which I had supposed full—were empty, and that (beyond odd tins of vegetables and meat, and some other matters) we had nothing on which to depend but the bread in the tank which I had already opened.

"After learning this I bestirred myself to do what I could, and set to work at fishing in the lagoon; but with no success. At this I was somewhat inclined to feel desperate until the thought came to me to try outside the lagoon, in the open sea.

"Here, at times, I caught odd fish; but so infrequently that they proved of but little help in keeping us from the hunger which threatened. It seemed to me that our deaths were likely to come by hunger, and not by the growth of the thing which had seized upon our bodies.

"We were in this state of mind when the fourth month wore out. Then I made a very horrible discovery. One morning, a little before midday, I came off from the ship with a portion of the biscuits which were left. In the mouth of her tent I saw my sweetheart sitting, eating something.

"'What is it, my dear?' I called out as I leaped ashore. Yet, on

hearing my voice, she seemed confused, and, turning, slyly threw something toward the edge of the little clearing. It fell short, and a vague suspicion having arisen within me, I walked across and picked it up. It was a piece of the gray fungus.

"As I went to her with it in my hand, she turned deadly pale; then a rose red.

"I felt strangely dazed and frightened.

"'My dear! My dear!' I said, and could say no more. Yet at my words she broke down and cried bitterly. Gradually, as she calmed, I got from her the news that she had tried it the preceding day, and—and liked it. I got her to promise on her knees not to touch it again, however great our hunger. After she had promised she told me that the desire for it had come suddenly, and that, until the moment of desire, she had experienced nothing toward it but the most extreme repulsion.

"Later in the day, feeling strangely restless, and much shaken with the thing which I had discovered, I made my way along one of the twisted paths—formed by the white, sandlike substance—

which led among the fungoid growth. I had, once before, ventured along there; but not to any great distance. This time, being involved in perplexing thought, I went much further than hitherto.

"Suddenly I was called to myself by a queer hoarse sound on my left. Turning quickly, I saw there was movement among an extraordinarily shaped mass of fungus, close to my elbow. It was swaying uneasily, as though it possessed life of its own. Abruptly, as I stared, the thought came to me that the thing had a grotesque resemblance to the figure of a distorted human creature. Even as the fancy flashed into my brain, there was a slight, sickening noise of tearing, and I saw that one of the branchlike arms was detaching itself from the surrounding gray masses, and coming toward me. The head of the thing—a shapeless gray ball—inclined in my direction. I stood stupidly, and the vile arm brushed across my face. I gave out a frightened cry and ran back a few paces. There was a sweetish taste upon my lips where the thing had touched me. I licked them, and was immediately filled with an inhuman desire. I turned and seized a mass of the fungus. Then more, and—more. I was insatiable. In the midst of devouring, the remembrance of the morning's discovery swept into my amazed brain. It was sent by God. I dashed the fragment I held to the ground. Then, utterly wretched and feeling a dreadful guiltiness, I made my way back to the little encampment.

"I think she knew, by some marvelous intuition which love must have given, as soon as she set eyes on me. Her quiet sympathy made it easier for me, and I told her of my sudden weakness; yet I omitted to mention the extraordinary thing which had gone before. I desired to spare her all unnecessary terror.

"But, for myself, I had added an intolerable knowledge, to breed an incessant terror in my brain; for I doubted not but that I had seen the end of one of these men who had come to the island in the ship in the lagoon; and in that monstrous ending I had seen our own.

"Thereafter we kept from the abominable food, though the

desire for it had entered into our blood. Yet our drear punishment was upon us; for, day by day, with monstrous rapidity, the fungoid growth took hold of our poor bodies. Nothing we could do would check it materially, and so—and so—we who had been human, became—Well, it matters less each day. Only—only we had been man and maid!

"And day by day the fight is more dreadful, to withstand the hunger-lust for the terrible lichen.

"A week ago we ate the last of the biscuit, and since that time I have caught three fish. I was out here fishing tonight when your schooner drifted upon me out of the mist. I hailed you. You know the rest, and may God, out of His great heart, bless you for your goodness to a—a couple of poor outcast souls."

There was the dip of an oar—another. Then the voice came again, and for the last time, sounding through the slight surrounding mist, ghostly and mournful.

"God bless you! Good-by!"

"Good-by," we shouted together, hoarsely, our hearts full of many emotions.

I glanced about me. I became aware that the dawn was upon us.

The sun flung a stray beam across the hidden sea, pierced the mist dully, and lit up the receding boat with a gloomy fire. Indistinctly I saw something nodding between the oars. I thought of a sponge—a great, gray nodding sponge—The oars continued to ply. They were gray—as was the boat—and my eyes searched a moment vainly for the conjunction of hand and oar. My gaze flashed back to the—head. It nodded forward as the oars went backward for the stroke. Then the oars were dipped, the boat shot out of the patch of light, and the—the thing went nodding into the mist.

Buggam Grange: A Good Old Ghost Story

STEPHEN LEACOCK

The evening was already falling as the vehicle in which I was contained entered upon the long and gloomy avenue that leads to Buggam Grange. A resounding shriek echoed through the wood as I entered the avenue. I paid no attention to it at the moment, judging it to be merely one of those resounding shrieks which one might expect to hear in such a place at such a time. As my drive continued, however, I found myself wondering in spite of myself why such a shriek should have been uttered at the very moment of my approach.

I am not by temperament in any degree a nervous man, and yet there was much in my surroundings to justify a certain feeling of apprehension. The Grange is situated in the loneliest part of England, the marsh country of the fens to which civilization has still hardly penetrated. The inhabitants, of whom there are only one and a half to the square mile, live here and there among the fens and eke out a miserable existence by frog fishing and catching flies. They speak a dialect so broken as to be practically unintelligible, while

the perpetual rain which falls upon them renders speech itself almost superfluous.

Here and there where the ground rises slightly above the level of the fens there are dense woods tangled with parasitic creepers and filled with owls. Bats fly from wood to wood. The air on the lower ground is charged with the poisonous gases which exude from the marsh, while in the woods it is heavy with the dank odors of deadly nightshade and poison ivy.

It had been raining in the afternoon, and as I drove up the avenue the mournful dripping of the rain from the dark trees accentuated the cheerlessness of the gloom. The vehicle in which I rode was a fly on three wheels, the fourth having apparently been broken and taken off, causing the fly to sag on one side and drag on its axle over the muddy ground, the fly thus moving only at a foot's pace in a way calculated to enhance the dreariness of the occasion. The driver on the box in front of me was so thickly muffled up as to be indistinguishable, while the horse which drew us was so thickly coated with mist as to be practically invisible. Seldom, I may say, have I had a drive of so mournful a character.

The avenue presently opened out upon a lawn with overgrown shrubberies and in the half darkness I could see the outline of the

Grange itself, a rambling, dilapidated building. A dim light struggled through the casement of a window in a tower room. Save for the melancholy cry of a row of owls sitting on the roof, and croaking of the frogs in the moat which ran around the grounds, the place was soundless. My driver halted his horse at the hither side of the moat. I tried in vain to urge him, by signs, to go further. I could see by the fellow's face that he was in a paroxysm of fear and indeed nothing but the extra sixpence which I had added to his fare would have made him undertake the drive up the avenue. I had no sooner alighted than he wheeled his cab about and made off.

Laughing heartily at the fellow's trepidation (I have a way of laughing heartily in the dark), I made my way to the door and pulled the bell-handle. I could hear the muffled reverberations of the bell far within the building. Then all was silent. I bent my ear to listen, but could hear nothing except perhaps the sound of a low moaning as of a person in pain or in great mental distress. Convinced, however, from what my friend Sir Jeremy Buggam had told me, that the Grange was not empty, I raised the ponderous knocker and beat with it loudly against the door.

But perhaps at this point I may do well to explain to my readers (before they are too frightened to listen to me) how I came to be beating on the door of Buggam Grange at nightfall on a gloomy November evening.

A year before I had been sitting with Sir Jeremy Buggam, the present baronet, on the verandah of his ranch in California.

"So you don't believe in the supernatural?" he was saying.

"Not in the slightest," I answered, lighting a cigar as I spoke. When I want to speak very positively, I generally light a cigar as I speak.

"Well, at any rate, Digby," said Sir Jeremy, "Buggam Grange is

haunted. If you want to be assured of it go down there anytime and spend the night and you'll see for yourself."

"My dear fellow," I replied, "nothing will give me greater pleasure. I shall be back in England in six weeks, and I shall be delighted to put your ideas to the test. Now tell me," I added somewhat cynically, "is there any particular season or day when your Grange is supposed to be specially terrible?"

Sir Jeremy looked at me strangely. "Why do you ask that?" he said. "Have you heard the story of the Grange?"

"Never heard of the place in my life," I answered cheerily. "Till you mentioned it tonight, my dear fellow, I hadn't the remotest idea that you still owned property in England."

"The Grange is shut up," said Sir Jeremy, "and has been for twenty years. But I keep a man there—Horrod—he was butler in my father's time and before. If you care to go, I'll write him that you're coming. And since you are taking your own fate in your hands, the fifteenth of November is the day."

At that moment Lady Buggam and Clara and the other girls came trooping out on the verandah, and the whole thing passed clean out of my mind. Nor did I think of it again until I was back in London. Then by one of those strange coincidences or premonitions—call it what you will—it suddenly occurred to me one morning that it was the fifteenth of November. Whether Sir Jeremy had written to Horrod or not, I did not know. But nonetheless nightfall found me, as I have described, knocking at the door of Buggam Grange.

The sound of the knocker had scarcely ceased to echo when I heard the shuffling of feet within, and the sound of chains and bolts being withdrawn. The door opened. A man stood before me holding a lighted candle which he shaded with his hand. His faded black clothes, once apparently a butler's dress, his white hair and advanced age left me in no doubt that he was Horrod of whom Sir Jeremy had spoken.

Without a word he motioned me to come in, and, still without speech, he helped me to remove my wet outer garments, and then beckoned me into a great room, evidently the dining room of the Grange.

I am not in any degree a nervous man by temperament, as I think I remarked before, and yet there was something in the vastness of the wainscotted room, lighted only by a single candle, and in the silence of the empty house, and still more in the appearance of my speechless attendant which gave me a feeling of distinct uneasiness. As Horrod moved to and fro I took occasion to scrutinize his face more narrowly. I have seldom seen features more calculated to inspire a nervous dread. The pallor of his face and the whiteness of his hair (the man was at least seventy), and still more the peculiar furtiveness of his eyes, seemed to mark him as one who lived under a great terror. He moved with a noiseless step and at times he turned his head to glance in the dark corners of the room.

"Sir Jeremy told me," I said, speaking as loudly and as heartily as I could, "that he would apprise you of my coming."

I was looking into his face as I spoke.

In answer Horrod laid his finger across his lips and I knew that he was deaf and dumb. I am not nervous (I think I said that), but the realization that my sole companion in the empty house was a deaf mute struck a cold chill to my heart.

Horrod laid in front of me a cold meat pie, a cold goose, a cheese and a tall flagon of cider. But my appetite was gone. I ate the goose, but found that after I had finished the pie I had but little zest for the cheese, which I finished without enjoyment. The cider had a sour taste, and after having permitted Horrod to refill the flagon twice, I found that it induced a sense of melancholy and decided to drink no more.

My meal finished, the butler picked up the candle and beckoned to me to follow him. We passed through the empty corridors of the house, a long line of pictured Buggams looking upon us as we passed, their portraits in the flickering light of the taper assuming a strange and life-like appearance as if leaning forward from their frames to gaze upon the intruder.

Horrod led me upstairs and I realized that he was taking me to the tower in the east wing in which I had observed a light.

The rooms to which the butler conducted me consisted of a sitting room with an adjoining bedroom, both of them fitted with antique wainscotting against which a faded tapestry fluttered. There was a candle burning on the table in the sitting room but its insufficient light only rendered the surroundings the more dismal. Horrod bent down in front of the fireplace and endeavored to light a fire there. But the wood was evidently damp, and the fire flickered feebly on the hearth.

The butler left me, and in the stillness of the house I could hear his shuffling step echo down the corridor. It may have been fancy, but it seemed to me that his departure was the signal for a low moan that came from somewhere behind the wainscot. There was a narrow cupboard door at one side of the room, and for the moment I wondered whether the moaning came from within. I am not as a rule lacking in courage (I am sure my reader will be decent enough to believe this), yet I found myself entirely unwilling to open the cupboard door and look within. In place of doing so I seated myself in a great chair in front of the feeble fire. I must have been seated there for some time when I happened to lift my eyes to the mantel above and saw, standing upon it, a letter addressed to myself. I knew the handwriting at once to be that of Sir Jeremy Buggam.

I opened it, and spreading it out within reach of the feeble candlelight, I read as follows:

My dear Digby,
In our talk you will remember I had no time to finish telling you about the mystery of Buggam Grange. I take for granted, however, that you will go there and that Horrod will put you in the tower rooms, which are the only ones that make any pretense of being habitable. I have, therefore, sent him this letter to deliver at the Grange itself. The story is this:

On the night of the fifteenth of November, fifty years ago, my grandfather was murdered in the room in which you are sitting, by his cousin Sir Duggam Buggam. He was stabbed from behind while seated at the little table at which you are probably reading this letter. The two had been playing cards at the table and my grandfather's body was found lying in a litter of cards and gold sovereigns on the floor. Sir Duggam Buggam, insensible from drink, lay beside him, the fatal knife at his hand, his fingers smeared with blood. My grandfather, though of the younger branch, possessed a part of the estates which were to revert to Sir Duggam on his death. Sir Duggam Buggam was tried at the Assizes and was hanged. On the day of his execution he was permitted by the authorities, out of respect for his rank, to wear a mask to the scaffold. The clothes in which he was executed are hanging at full length in the little cupboard to your right, and the mask is above them. It is said that on every fifteenth of November at midnight the cupboard door opens and Sir Duggam Buggam walks out into the room. It has been found impossible to get servants to remain at the Grange, and the place—except for the presence of Horrod—has been unoccupied for a generation. At the time of the murder Horrod was a young man of twenty-two, newly entered into the service of the family. It was he who entered the room and discovered the crime. On the day of the execution he was stricken with paralysis

and has never spoken since. From that time to this he has never consented to leave the Grange where he lives in isolation.

Wishing you a pleasant night after your tiring journey,

I remain,
Very faithfully,
Jeremy Buggam

I leave my reader to imagine my state of mind when I completed the perusal of the letter.

I have as little belief in the supernatural as anyone, yet I must confess that there was something in the surroundings in which I now found myself which rendered me at least uncomfortable. My reader may smile if he will, but I assure him that it was with a very distinct feeling of uneasiness that I at length managed to rise to my feet and, grasping my candle in my hand, to move backward into the bedroom. As I backed into it something so like a moan seemed to proceed from the closed cupboard that I accelerated my backward movement to a considerable degree. I hastily blew out the candle, threw myself upon the bed and drew the bed clothes over my head, keeping, however, one eye and one ear still out and available.

How long I lay thus listening to every sound, I cannot tell. The stillness had become absolute. From time to time I could dimly hear the distant cry of an owl and once far away in the building below a sound as of someone dragging a chain along a floor. More than once I was certain that I heard the sound of moaning behind the wainscot. Meantime I realized that the hour must now be drawing close upon the fatal moment of midnight. My watch I could not see in the darkness, but by reckoning the time that must have elapsed I knew that midnight could not be far away. Then presently my ear, alert to every sound, could just distinguish far away across the fens the striking of a church bell, in the clock tower of Buggam village church, no doubt, tolling the hour of twelve.

On the last stroke of twelve, the cupboard door in the next room opened. There is no need to ask me how I knew it. I couldn't, of course, see it, but I could hear, or sense in some way, the sound of it. I could feel my hair, all of it, rising upon my head. I was aware that there was a *presence* in the adjoining room, I will not say a person, a living soul, but a *presence*. Anyone who has been in the next room to a presence will know just how I felt. I could hear a sound as of someone groping on the floor and the faint rattle as of coins.

My hair was now perpendicular. My reader can blame it or not, but it was.

Then at this very moment from somewhere below in the building there came the sound of a prolonged and piercing cry, a cry as of a soul passing in agony. My reader may censure me or not, but right at this moment I decided to beat it. Whether I should have remained to see what was happening is a question that I will not discuss. My one idea was to get out and to get out quickly. The window of the tower room was some twenty-five feet above the ground. I sprang out through the casement in one leap and landed on the grass below. I jumped over the shrubbery in one bound and cleared the moat in one jump. I went down the avenue in about six strides and ran five miles along the road through the fens in three minutes. This at least is an accurate transcription of my sensations. It may have taken longer. I never stopped till I found myself on the threshold of the Buggam Arms in Little Buggam, beating on the door for the landlord.

I returned to Buggam Grange on the next day in the bright sunlight of a frosty November morning, in a seven cylinder motor car with six local constables and a physician. It makes all the difference. We carried revolvers, spades, pickaxes, shotguns and a ouija board.

What we found cleared up forever the mystery of the Grange. We discovered Horrod the butler lying on the dining room floor quite dead. The physician said that he had died from heart failure. There was evidence from the marks of his shoes in the dust that he had come in the night to the tower room. On the table he had placed a paper which contained a full confession of his having murdered Jeremy Buggam fifty years before. The circumstances of the murder had rendered it easy for him to fasten the crime upon Sir Duggam, already insensible from drink. A few minutes with the ouija board enabled us to get a full corroboration from Sir Duggam. He promised, moreover, now that his name was cleared, to go away from the premises forever.

My friend, the present Sir Jeremy, has rehabilitated Buggam Grange. The place is rebuilt. The moat is drained. The whole house is lit with electricity. There are beautiful motor drives in all directions in the woods. He has had the bats shot and the owls stuffed. His daughter, Clara Buggam, became my wife. She is looking over my shoulder as I write. What more do you want?

The End

An Excerpt from . . .

The Devil's Thoughts

SAMUEL TAYLOR COLERIDGE

I

From his brimstone bed at break of day
A walking the Devil is gone,
To visit his snug little farm the Earth
And see how his stock goes on.

II

Over the hill and over the dale,
And he went over the plain,
And backward and forward he switched his long tail
As a gentleman switches his cane.

III

And how then was the Devil drest?
Oh! he was in his Sunday's best:
His jacket was red and his breeches were blue,
And there was a hole where the tail came through.

Acknowledgments

"Jimmy Takes Vanishing Lessons" from *Jimmy Takes Vanishing Lessons* by Walter R. Brooks. Copyright © 1965 by Walter R. Brooks. Reprinted by permission of the estate of Dorothy R. Brooks.

"Of a Promise Kept" from *In Ghostly Japan* by Lafcadio Hearn (1899).

"The Storm" by Jules Verne (1828–1905).

"The Legend of Sleepy Hollow" from *The Sketch Book of Geoffrey Crayon, Gent.* by Washington Irving (1820).

"The Cremation of Sam McGee" from *Songs of a Sourdough* by Robert Service. Copyright © 1907 by Robert Service. Reprinted by permission of M.Wm. Krasilovsky.

"The Hand" by Guy de Maupassant from *The Dark Side of Maupassant*, selected and translated by Dr. Arnold Kellett. Copyright © 1989 by Arnold Kellett. Reprinted by permission of Xanadu Publications Ltd.

"The Golden Arm," traditional English fairy tale based on Joseph Jacobs's version in *English Fairy Tales* (1890).

"My Grandfather, Hendry Watty" by Sir Arthur Quiller-Couch (1863–1944).

"Huw" from *The Obstinate Ghost and Other Ghostly Tales* by Geoffrey Palmer and Noel Lloyd. Copyright © 1974 by Geoffrey Palmer and Noel Lloyd. Reprinted by permission of Odhams Press.

"The Visitor" from *Scary Poems for Rotten Kids* by Sean O'Huigin. Copyright © 1988 by sean o huigin. Reprinted by permission of Black Moss Press.

"King o' the Cats," traditional English fairy tale based on Joseph Jacobs's version in *English Fairy Tales* (1890).

"Best Before" by Laurie Channer. Copyright © 1998 by Laurie Channer. Published by permission of the author.

"The Blackstairs Mountain" from *A Book of Witches* by Ruth Manning-Sanders. Copyright © 1965 by Ruth Manning-Sanders. Reprinted by permission of Methuen Children's Books.

"Climax for a Ghost Story" from *Visitations* by I. A. Ireland (1919).

"Dracula's Guest" by Bram Stoker (1847–1912).

"A Change of Aunts" from *Ghostly Companions* by Vivien Alcock. Copyright © 1984 by Vivien Alcock. Reprinted by permission of Methuen Children's Books.

"The Strange Visitor," traditional English fairy tale based on Joseph Jacobs's version in *English Fairy Tales* (1890).

"The Monkey's Paw" by W. W. Jacobs (1902).

"The Train Room" by Gary Hines.

"The Geebung Polo Club" from *The Man from Snowy River and Other Verses* by Banjo Paterson (1895).

"The Doll's Ghost" by Marion Crawford (1854–1909).

"Lizard: The Devil's Plaything" by Karen Voss Peters. Copyright © 1998 by Karen Voss Peters. Published by permission of the author.

"The Ride-by-Nights" from *The Complete Poems of Walter de la Mare* by Walter de la Mare. Copyright © 1969 (USA: 1970) by The Literary Trustees of Walter de la Mare and the Society of Authors as their representative.

"The Kit-Bag" by Algernon Blackwood.

"The Pocket" from *Scary Poems for Rotten Kids* by Sean O'Huigin. Copyright © 1988 by sean o huigin. Reprinted by permission of Black Moss Press.

"The Story-Teller" by Saki (1870–1916).

"John Charrington's Wedding" by E. Nesbit (1858–1924).

"The Voice in the Night" from *The House on the Borderland* by William Hope Hodgson (1908).

"Buggam Grange: A Good Old Ghost Story" by Stephen Leacock (1869–1944).

"The Devil's Thoughts" by Samuel Taylor Coleridge (1772–1834).

Every reasonable effort has been made to contact copyright holders; any errors or omissions in the above list are entirely unintentional. If notified, the publisher will be pleased to make any necessary corrections at the earliest opportunity.